# ZOMBACTER

## CENTER CITY CONTAGION

PATRICK SEAN BINGHAM

www.severedpress.com

This novel is a work of fiction. Names, characters, places and incidents are the product of the author's imagination, or are used fictitiously. Any resemblance to actual events, locales or persons, living or dead, is purely coincidental.

ISBN: 978-0-9871044-7-2

# CONTENTS

# ACKNOWLEDGMENTS

I have many people to thank for making this novel a reality:

My Beta Readers: David Hull, Phillip Banta, Carl and Kit Burdick, Cody Buller, and Aubrey Humbolt, for bringing this book, and all its characters, back from the dead (pun intended).

Fellow writers: David Hull and Jeff Hall, for pushing me to publish *Zombacter*.

Gary Lucas, Romana Baotic, and the editors at Severed Press, for unleashing *Zombacter* upon the world.

All my friends, for inspiring me to write.

Bill Blair, for our conversations regarding the zombie genre's missing scientific plausibility.

Last but not least, my family: Lexi, Devin, and Joani, for enduring countless hours of tortuous conversation about zombies and for being the first beta Readers. Thank you, thank you, and thank you.

# PROLOGUE

Carl Wurling took a detour on his way to work that evening. He was already late for his shift but his stomach was growling from the pain of not having eaten anything the night before. The E.R. had been jam-packed every night the last couple of weeks and he was looking forward to getting a break. It was Friday and soon it would be Thompson's turn at the helm. Now the smell of fresh food was too much to bear. Frustrated by all the roadblocks, he parked his car on 12th Street near Terminal Market in Center City, Philadelphia. The heavy aroma of Chinese food was mixed with the foul odors wafting up from beneath the sewer grates in the sidewalk. Although the odor seemed particularly strong that evening, Carl was too hungry to give it much thought. In fact, he wasn't thinking about much of anything until someone bumped into him as they ran past. Looking up he saw another man approaching from the shadows of an alley to ask for spare change, or so he thought.

He had his usual line on the tip of his tongue, *Sorry buddy I don't have any change*, when searing pain tore through his body.

No man should ever have to live through what Carl Wurling was about to experience, but then again, Carl wouldn't live through it either.

It made no sense to him. Ruben and Jennifer had worked with the lab animals all semester and they were fine.

*Why is Professor Northrop making me get tested for...whatever's wrong with the animals? I've never even actually touched one of them, not without gloves anyway,* Blaine thought to himself as he walked down the pale-green hallway of the Potterfield Bioengineering building.

He was sure they were just trying to get him to quit after the incident with the rabbits.

*It wasn't my fault. Nobody told me not to put them in the trash, nobody! Dr. Langley had that look on his face when he told me to get rid of them and I wasn't about to lose my internship over some stupid dead rabbits. Damn rabbits! What else was I supposed to do with them?* he thought.

"Oh man, my dad's gonna kill me," Blaine whimpered as he trudged down the stairs leading to the lab.

He stopped suddenly before reaching the door leading to the 1st floor. He was frozen in place by shock and disbelief at the sight of something his mind simply couldn't grasp. Still staring at the scene unfolding before him, Blaine mumbled one word before he could think not too.

"Rubes?"

And then, it saw Blaine.

The morning had yet to arrive and Sheriff Roy Clay stood alone outside the gas station in the Arizona desert. He stared at his blood-spattered hands.

"What have I done?"

But Roy already knew the answer to that question. His anguish was beyond the capacity of any human to bear, as he understood the full meaning of his previous visions.

He was a murderer and hopelessly insane. The sheriff fell to his knees on the sidewalk outside the store. He didn't know how all this had happened but it had. Even if there was a treatment for his kind of mental illness, he knew there was no cure for the guilt that overwhelmed him. Roy just couldn't live with it. He looked up into the night sky one last time. It was so beautiful, so full of stars. With a shaking hand, he put the revolver to his temple. His last thoughts were of his deputy Joy Ferguson. Roy would've married a girl like that. They had so much in common.

# THE BEGINNING OF THE END

**October 12:**

The Potterfield bioengineering building faced 34th street in Philadelphia and although it wasn't located in the most serene setting, it was close enough to the ball field to provide easy access to sporting events. Like the majority of buildings sprouting from the concrete of this city, its front was mostly green glass. This allowed light to penetrate its gloomy interior.

Deep within this edifice in a forgotten corner of its lowest floor was a laboratory with no windows. Inside of it, there was a seemingly odd assortment of various-sized animal cages neatly stacked on top of one another against the stark white walls. A strange clicking sound emanated from a large fume hood taking up one corner of the room. Un-patterned, white floor-tile abutted a single row of black shoe molding at the base of the wall, offering little to please the eye.

Clearly, this wasn't a tranquil place to study the goings-on of nature. The white tubes and red-blue striped wiring that ran among the enclosures were the tendons, arteries, and veins the professor used to ration life to the lab animals. Rabbits, mice, snakes, birds, and a plethora of more exotic creatures were bathed in flashes of unnatural light and sound emitted by the computers and menacing, stainless-steel equipment surrounding the cages.

Near the center of the lab and placed where one could walk around them were black phenolic countertops that stood atop plain wooden cabinets and drawers. On top of these were racks that held semi-inverted test tubes, beakers, and flasks.

Within the recesses of the test facility and across from the only entrance was a mundane storeroom housing older equipment, file boxes, cleaning supplies, and an emergency shower. Off to its right was the dissection chamber whose pale, greenish-white walls could be seen through a single window that began halfway up from the floor. Unlike the black countertops that lay in the center of the main room, stainless steel countertops with fume hoods ran the length of these walls. An awful, round drain was set in the middle of the sagging gray floor to catch any bodily fluids that might escape the edges of the cold, steel dissecting table. In this grisly place, experiments ended or in some cases began. Jake Northrop enjoyed working in the solitude of this incongruent environment. It was his life and for the most part, the cold flicker of fluorescent lighting suited his demeanor.

Things had been good for Jake ever since the University secured a contract with Nanotech to develop the bio-computer, a nanotechnology driven, lightning-fast machine far superior to traditional silicon-based computers in every way. The money that flowed into his department was more than anyone had seen.

Yes, bio-computers were the way of the future and Jake wanted to be the first to build one. Scientists had already developed rudimentary microchips from rat neurons. These were small, inefficient, had little computing power, and were only good so long as the rat neurons survived. All this was child's play to Jake Northrop. Besides it'd already been done. Something new, something better had to be developed before the dream of a useful bio-computer could be realized. The world was waiting.

Jake's first breakthrough came right on schedule. He was able to genetically modify the common garden-variety bacteria called Geobacter to adsorb various metallic ions. The bacteria would then spontaneously align with the electric field of an electronic circuit and become part of it. However, he wasn't using just any electronic circuit. What set Jake's plan for a bio-computer apart from the mundane experiments appearing in science journals was the fact that his circuits were made from living rabbit brains. More impressive was the fact that his circuits continued functioning long after the bacteria were dead and had been isolated from the rabbit.

Jake sat at his desk desperately trying to finish typing in grades. The sun had long-since disappeared before his final keystroke. He looked at his watch and muttered a curse before dashing out of his cramped office at the University. Jake was immersed in his thoughts as he raced down the empty corridors on his way to the lab. By his own account, he should've been there hours ago but it was well after mid-terms and he was finally forced to spend a day tabulating student grades. Irritated that his teaching responsibilities were slowing his progress on the bio-computer, he berated himself for going into academia. He was even more frustrated by the fact he couldn't go anywhere else and have the sort of freedoms he now enjoyed. Jake stood impatiently at the elevator for only a few seconds before he decided to take the stairs down to the lab. As he trotted down the final steps he literally ran into one of his student assistants, knocking her books out of her hands.

"Oh I'm sorry Jennifer! I was in a hurry to get to…"

"The lab? Yeah my dad's waiting for you."

Jake exhaled deeply and shut his eyes.

"How long has he been waiting?"

"Long enough professor. You should go."

"Thanks, sorry about the…I'll see you tomorrow," Jake yelled over his shoulder as he ran toward the lab.

Jake skidded to a halt in front of the lab door, took a deep breath and smoothed his hair down before opening it.

Ronald Langley, the Dean of Science, sat in Jake's chair drumming his fingers on the desk. Jake was instantly annoyed but suppressed the emotion well enough that it never registered on his face.

"Ron, good to see you again!" Jake announced with artificial surprise.

"Don't start that crap with me Northrop. I've got better things to do than wait around here for you all day. You were supposed to meet me here over an hour ago!"

Jake suddenly remembered the appointment but it was too late to do anything about it.

"Mid-terms Ron… I got tied up. Look I'm sorry."

"Enough - just show me the progress you've made on my bio-computer."

"Okay, take a look at these screen captures I took yesterday… Ron, it works. The process I've developed is going to make the bio-computer a reality. Look at the bacteria, see how well they behave."

"Holy crap, will you look at this! They've completely aligned themselves with the neural network!" Ronald Langley couldn't believe his eyes as he stared into the computer screen at the images of glowing green bacteria coating the rabbit's brain cells.

"And this is just the beginning. In a few months I'll have something extraordinary to show the world," Jake mused.

The smile on his face accentuated the deepening wrinkles around the corners of his mouth and brilliant blue eyes. Jake resembled a young Kurt Russell and still managed a youthful appearance at the age of forty-six. On several occasions, he was forced to delicately maneuver around some of his infatuated female students.

"I'm not simply talking about a bio-computer here Ron."

"What do you mean?"

"I mean artificial intelligence."

"That's the kinda talk that crackpot Minsky used to spout. He was a dreamer Jake. None of his artificial intelligence research was grounded in reality. You need to keep your eyes on the prize. Forget that artificial intelligence crap."

"He wasn't a crackpot. MIT didn't think so and neither do I. He was just a little before his time and didn't have a bio-computer available. No machine is capable of doing what my creation can."

"Maybe you're just as nutty as he was. Anyway, how the hell did you get them to colonize the network without killing the rabbit?" asked Langley, his balding head beaded with sweat.

"Ah, ancient Chinese secret."

"Damn it Jake!"

"Easy, I'm just messing with you. The bacteria don't feed off of their neurons. They use the nutrients I provide instead. I inject the rabbits with low concentrations of nanoparticle-bound heavy metals combined with immunosuppressant drugs. I've been able to set up a symbiotic relationship among the rabbits and the bacteria. Initially, I have to suppress their immune systems but the bacteria are able to take over that responsibility after they settle in. The trick is getting the bacteria started," Jake explained.

"Sounds time consuming… and expensive," Langley said.

“These things always take time for the kinks to be worked out. Anyway, to keep the process going after the drug therapy, I’ve engineered the bacteria to activate the pleasure center in the brain and continue to suppress the immune system at the same time.”

“So the rabbit gets a reward for allowing the bacteria to stay?”

“Exactly, I got the idea from a fungus that induces behavior alterations in insects to ensure spore transmittal to another host. You see there’s this caterpillar that…”

“Get to the point Jake,” Langley remarked irritably.

“Okay, um… I combined genetic material from a protist, which is known to suppress the immune system of its host, with *Geobacter*. But I selected genes that wouldn’t harm the rabbits,” said Jake, smiling.

“And that’s important why?” Langley asked.

“Well, these bacteria can trick their host into allowing them to stay even though they don’t belong there. In this case there doesn’t seem to be any harm to the rabbits.”

Langley shook his head. “My first question is, how they hell are you going to put a rabbit into a laptop Jake?”

“Very funny Ron. After the network has been completely overlain with bacteria, we’ll harvest them. The spider-silk genes I’ve added to the bacteria will help bind them together and I can monitor their progress using a gene that makes them fluoresce green.”

“Harvest them. Like picking apples, you just harvest them?” Langley asked.

“Not exactly, the rabbits have to die to harvest the networks,” Jake said while wincing.

“So let me get this straight. You engineer this stuff, all tree-hugger-like, so it won’t hurt the rabbits and now you’re gonna smack ‘em over the head and rip their brains out? That’ll be a P.R. nightmare if P.E.T.A. ever gets wind of it.”

“Eventually we’ll grow cultured brain cells in the lab and won’t need the live rabbits anymore. But until I find a way of quickly growing an entire brain in a Petri dish this is the only way to keep them alive long enough for the bacteria to completely coat all the neural networks.

“We need to keep all this under wraps for now. I don’t want anyone finding out what you’re up to,” Langley stated after glancing around to make sure no one else was nearby.

“Little late for that don’t you think?”

“Late for what?” Langley’ eyebrows lowered as he glared at Jake.

“I’m using student interns Ron! They can’t keep secrets. If you’re worried about that, get me lab assistants with credentials instead of relying on kids.”

“So you want me to cut your salary and hire a couple scientists?”

“That’s not fair. We’re talking about something that’ll revolutionize the world. Think of it, computers that can process data intelligently for a change and at lightning speed!”

“Yeah, yeah, you just make sure those bacteria won’t be a problem and I’ll make sure you have plenty of students to help build my computer.” Langley stated while looking up at Jake, at 5’5’’ Langley had to look up to most people, and he didn’t like it one bit.

“Our immune system should be able to take care of them,” replied Jake confidently.

“Should?” Langley asked while turning red in the face.

“What I mean is that there’s no need to conduct any tests. My bacteria aren’t capable of infecting humans,” Jake blurted.

Langley scowled at Jake.

“If it’ll make you feel better I’ll look into it, alright?”

“You’d damn well better. I’ve got the President of the University, CEOs, stock holders, and a whole list of other jerks all breathing down my neck so don’t screw this one up! The goddamn Japanese are working on a friggin’ optical system, the Russians claim they have a quantum computer and the French….well they have some kind of weird-ass parallel dimension thing they’re working on and they’re all ahead of us!” Langley yelled as he slammed the door behind him.

Jake heaved a sigh of relief. Now that Langley was gone he could get some work done. Jake smiled.

*Parallel dimensions, Ron had no idea what he was talking about*, he chuckled to himself and then began a full-on belly laugh, the kind of laugh that happens between friends.

Jake made his way over to the rabbit cages. "All right buddy, it's time to get your old room-mate back," he told Barney.

He placed Algernon back into the cage with Barney.

"There you are. I'll start your treatments again tomorrow. Don't look at me like that. I didn't take much, just a little of the old gray stuff and not from any place important. You'll be good as new in a day or so."

Jake always liked animals and he imagined that he treated the ones in his lab no differently than he would a person. Jake frowned suddenly and then shook his head.

*Ah, there's no way this stuff could infect people. It took a ton of immunosuppressant drugs to allow the bacteria to get a foothold in the rabbit,* He dismissed the thought.

"Nighty-night, boys."

And with that, Jake turned out the lights in the lab and left for home.

A figure had waited in the shadows for Jake to leave his laboratory. A few minutes later someone was hastily transferring small quantities of the genetically altered *Geobacter* from several vials into a single glass tube. This robbery had been carefully orchestrated over several weeks with help from a rival organization and now the time had come. Simple espionage wouldn't do the trick. Reproducing from scratch the bacteria that Jake had carefully cultivated over the past three years would be too time-consuming. The person knew that the rewards for stealing Jake's bacteria for another company would be very worthwhile indeed. Even so, the nervous robber considered backing out of the whole deal at the last moment. But the allure of easy money won the day.

Working too quickly in the darkened laboratory, the individual accidentally knocked over one of the vials. The liquid was clumsily siphoned up off of the counter top and squirted back into its original container. After it had been refilled, the inept robber continued to work until the quota was satisfied. The thief cracked open the laboratory door and stole one last look to see if anyone was out in the hall and then crept out of the Potterfield science building. The shadowy figure leapt into a dark-green, weather-beaten sedan parked in the adjacent lot and sped away unnoticed.

It was raining the following morning when a small package labeled *Fragile-Glass*, was delivered to the post office for shipment to Krattatech Industries in New York City. A postal clerk carefully placed the package in a separate bin. Another worker who didn't see the tiny box, inadvertently tossed a much heavier package, addressed to Mr. Daniel Morton of San Diego, California, directly on top of it. An hour later someone noticed a few wet packages and thinking the ordinary-looking liquid was simply rain, dutifully wiped them dry. All the packages sent from the post office that day made it to their destinations.

**October 22:**

The air in Philadelphia was usually cool and crisp this time of year. By now, the leaves had normally turned brilliant shades of gold, orange, and crimson. This year was different. It was unusually warm, humid and overcast, which allowed swarms of biting insects to plague city dwellers every out of doors moment. There always seemed to be smog veiling the tops of the buildings and the few remaining leaves simply hung dead, brown, and lifeless on the trees. Some people blamed the lack of autumn color on the drought, but most people barely noticed or simply didn't care.

Franklin King was a sanitation worker in the city and he noticed the changes in the weather. Frank, as his friends called him, noticed the changes in people's moods and blamed that on the weather as well. He usually liked his job but today he just wanted to crawl back into bed with his wife and sleep off this gloomy feeling. If he had to be at work, he would rather be on the landfill crew. It smelled badly but it was like looking at the city through the perspective of an archaeologist. He was able to see what people ate, what they bought, and what they threw away. His mind could wander there.

His favorite thing to do was to watch a family of foxes that lived around the dump. Whenever he had the chance, he would bring them scraps of food from Terminal Market. The male fox would let him get fairly close and that always made him feel good. But on this day and indeed most days Frank just rode through Center City on the back of the blue and yellow garbage truck. At least that way he could feel the wind blowing on his face. Lately there hadn't been much wind from Mother Nature and when there was a breeze it was never refreshing. Although Frank liked the outdoors, he was bored of riding around the city. There wasn't much for him to do except pick up refuse that didn't make it into the compactor and that didn't occur very often. To take his mind off of his plight, he spoke to the shop keepers. It made him feel better on the inside, especially if he could brighten their day with something he said.

"How you doin' Mr. O'Leary? You still got that little Chihuahua…what's-his-name…Mr. Skittles?" Frank called out to a store owner sweeping the sidewalk.

"Hey Frank! That you back there? I thought you were leaving us."

The man looked over his shoulder toward his shop and yelled, "Come here boy! Come say hello to Frank!" The tiny dog ran out of the shop, hopped into his master's arms, and licked his face.

"That's a good boy!" the man said to the dog while smiling.

"What do you think Frank? Was it a good trade? My ex got the house and I got the dog."

Frank shrugged his shoulders and asked, "You happy?"

"Best thing that ever happened to me!" the man said to Frank as the truck was driving away.

"I know that's right!" Frank yelled back as they rounded the corner, and on they drove. For now, Frank could only hope for the day to end so that the weekend would be here.

Ruben struggled to separate them.

"Oh Christ man, he's chewing his leg off!" Ruben yelled to Jennifer who had just walked into the lab.

"What's happening?" Jennifer shouted.

"I don't know. They're fighting. I can't tell which one is… son of a bitch! The little bastard just bit right through my glove!"

"Oh my God, are you okay?" Jennifer asked, visibly shaken.

"No! He bit me damn it. I was trying to keep the other one from killing him and he bit me!"

"He was probably just scared Ruben."

"Look, they stopped fighting," said Ruben rather incredulously.

"Barney's hurt, Ruben. Look at his leg."

"I know, I know. How's the other one?" asked Ruben while examining his hand.

"The other one is called Algernon and he has blood all over him. I can't tell. It looks like he…oh gross!"

"Oh shit, his guts are hanging out. We'd better go get Professor Northrop," Ruben said as he ran out of the lab.

Jennifer followed him to the elevator and they waited in silence as the elevator made its way down to the ground floor. Ruben's sandy-brown hair fell into his green eyes and he absentmindedly brushed it out of his face with his injured hand.

"Ouch, I almost forgot about that," he said while wincing.

"You'd better get some antibiotics for that. You might even need stitches," said Jennifer, finally breaking the silence.

"I'll need more than that if Dr. Langley hears about this."

"Why are you so afraid of my dad? You're always trying to kiss his ..."

"Don't say it. You know why Jen. I need this job. I have bills to pay. I've got a car, I have insurance premiums and...I have you."

Ruben pressed her back against the wall and ran his hand up her leg when suddenly the door to the elevator opened.

"Jesus!" exclaimed Ruben.

"You big baby, you're a little jumpy aren't you?" Jennifer asked while grinning. "Come on tiger we've gotta go get the professor," she cooed as she walked backwards into the elevator while twisting a strand of her blond hair around her finger.

"I won't need this job forever you know. I have a plan that's going to make me—us a lot of money and then we can do whatever we want. We won't have to worry about your dad anymore," Ruben said with a grin.

"What plan? What are you talking about? Did you get a job somewhere else?"

"I'm not telling you just yet. You'll see."

Jake was typing an e-mail when his two young assistants burst through the door. "Dr. Northrop you've gotta come downstairs. Something's happened with the rabbits!" Ruben exclaimed.

Jake looked over the screen of his laptop and asked worriedly, "What's happened?"

"You've just gotta see for yourself."

"Come on!" Jennifer urged.

"All right calm down. Is your hand bleeding Ruben?" Jake asked, while following his interns out of his office.

"Yeah, it's not bad. I'll be all right," Ruben said casually, making every attempt to sound manlier than he really was.

On the way down to the lab Jake asked them again what had transpired. They explained the situation to Jake and now he was really worried.

"So that is how you found them today, fighting?" asked Jake.

Ruben explained, "Yes, I came in and I heard one of them or maybe both of them, you know, like, screaming and I ran over to see what was happening and the rest is like we've told you already."

"Well they're not fighting now," said Jake, as he stared at the rabbits.

"I know but look at his stomach," Ruben motioned over to Algernon.

"I think Barney's missing a leg too," added Jennifer, looking quite nauseous.

"I can see that," retorted Jake. "Man, what would cause them to do this to one another?" He mumbled to himself.

"I'm going to have to euthanize Algernon. Barney might be okay but, he won't be able to hop like he used to. Give me a hand here Ruben. Just hold the noose like this. Good, now I'll just slip this around him and voilà."

They removed Barney from the cage he shared with Algernon and put him into a cage of his own.

"I'll have to tend to that leg in a minute. Right now I need to put Algernon down. I don't want him to suffer any more that he already has," said Jake rather remorsefully.

Jake took the entire cage and sat it beneath the large fume hood in the corner. He placed a large plastic container over the top of the cage and attached a hose to the fitting protruding from its side. He opened the valve and walked away from the fume hood and toward his students.

Northrop placed his hands on their shoulders and said, "It'll all be over in just few minutes guys. I'm sorry you had to witness this. And Ruben, go get that hand checked out."

"Yes, sir," replied Ruben, still staring at his hand.

"Jennifer, help me patch up Barney and then you can call it a night okay?"

"All right professor," Jennifer said with a hint of resignation in her voice.

She turned to face Ruben and said worriedly, "Ruben call me and let me know how it went at the hospital, okay?"

Ruben nodded before leaving.

The hospital was brightly lit and located in the heart of Philly. The front of the building was a technological façade of concrete, steel, and mirrored glass. Although it lacked the welcoming warmth of a country abode, it offered hope to those who entered its doors. Normally the hospital wasn't busy but then again things hadn't been normal since the weather had changed.

Heather's shift had just begun and already she was tired. It's wasn't because of the increase in patient load; it was just that she didn't feel well and hadn't been sleeping much. It was difficult getting used to working in the evenings after having been on the day shift for the past year. On the upside, the hospital wasn't far from Terminal Market and she could get good food before they closed in the evenings. She still hated working in the E.R. but that's where Carl was working, so she had those little moments of forbidden love to look forward to. It was strange; she used to feel that way about Jake too. She wondered for a moment exactly when all that had changed and why. It didn't matter now. She had a new life and a new lover, one that was there for her when she needed him. Suddenly, she realized she was gripping the edge of the desk and frowned through long, curly locks of chestnut-colored hair.

"Oh, that man has always put me in a bad mood," she said to herself as she stormed off down the hall.

That wasn't entirely true. Once upon a time Heather and Jake had been happy together. However, Jake was only truly happy when he was solving problems, conducting research. He tried to warn Heather about his obsessive-compulsive nature when they had first met but as they say, love is blind and so is youth. Now all Heather could remember were the bad times, the lonely times and how the tall, dark, and handsome Carl had rescued her from a life of boredom.

Carl was a good man, an honest man, and a dedicated doctor who was always willing to help out in the E.R. That's why he agreed to pull the graveyard shift for the next month. It's also the reason his wife left him. It was hard on him. He loved his two children dearly and would tear up when thinking about them. He thought about them often. But Carl wasn't a sad or a lonely man. He was truly quite funny at times. His ex-wife always loved that one thing about him. It was also why Heather fell in love with him.

"Oh my Heather, what would I do without you?" Carl smiled as he asked himself the question.

*I am one lucky man,* he concluded.

Carl was indeed lucky. His family wasn't wealthy, unlike most of his peers. Even with a scholarship, he had to work his way through medical school. Although he didn't graduate at the top of his class, he was well respected by the faculty and could count more friends than enemies among his classmates.

Carl came from a loving family and it showed. His father was a car salesman in New Jersey and his mother was a seamstress. They loved their three sons but Carl had always been their favorite. The Wurlings knew their youngest son Carl was destined for great things. Once when he was only seven years old, a neighbor's dog attacked the family cat. They didn't have enough money to take it to a vet, so Carl sewed its wounds together and nursed it back to health.

Carl was well suited to the practice of medicine, everybody thought so, and yet he was just as handy with a wrench. He was gifted that way. Carl possessed the upper body strength of a blacksmith but his hands were nimble and steady. He could've easily been a fine neurosurgeon but he chose general practice instead. He felt he could help more people that way.

Dr. Wurling's biggest flaw was that he neglected his own family. In fact, he was usually so consumed by his work that he ignored everyone even when he wasn't working. It was sad that he could help so many people but he could never help himself. Carl was many things but above all else he was always sincere.

Jake and Jennifer had finished taking care of Barney about an hour ago and Jennifer had already left when Jake remembered Algernon. As he approached the fume hood he thought he heard something.

*It sounded like…no it couldn't be,* thought Jake.

He lifted the fume hood and then raised the plastic container. To his amazement, Algernon was slowly dragging himself around in circles.

"My God, this strain of Geobacter must act like some sort of healing agent on…" but Jake stopped short when he saw the contents of Algernon's abdomen trailing behind him.

He now knew something was very wrong. He came in for a closer look and he could see Algernon's glazed eyes. The rabbit's mouth hung open revealing dark congealed blood. Jake tapped on his cage and Algernon continued moving in circles. When he picked up the cage, Algernon exploded to the side where Jake's fingers were poking through. Jake panicked and dropped it on the floor. The rabbit let out a gurgling scream and bounced around the cage flinging his intestinal contents all over the room.

"Jesus Christ!" Jake spluttered while covering his face.

Jake washed himself off in the emergency shower and then put on his biohazard suit. He was determined to find out what had gone wrong with the experiment. This time he approached the cage with more caution and picked it up using the metal pole with a noose on its end. He set it down on the table and then shot Algernon with a tranquilizer dart. He didn't go down. He shot him again, and then a third time, a fourth time, and still no effect. Algernon looked like a bloody dartboard but continued to move in circles around the cage.

*I don't understand. Is Geobacter responsible for this? Could it be stimulating the rabbit's brain, keeping it going like this? This is absolutely awful. I've got to put this poor thing out of its misery,* thought Jake.

He hefted the straight-edged shovel used for cleaning up animal waste and brought it down through the top of the cage and through Algernon's neck. There was very little blood. Algernon's mouth opened and closed incessantly. Jake felt sick to his stomach but couldn't turn away from the spectacle before him. Once again, the animal's body began moving in circles. Jake pondered his next move for what seemed like an eternity before making his decision. Using the metal pole, he took hold of the cage once more and placed it back underneath the fume hood.

"I have to find out what's causing this," Jake said to himself.

He unlatched the cage and reached for Algernon's body with metal tongs. The rabbit's body writhed and kicked as the tongs collapsed around its mangled remains. Jake walked quickly over to a large metal cylinder containing liquid nitrogen. He opened the lid and immersed the still violently wriggling body into its cryogenic tomb. The liquid boiled violently and the flailing of the animal's body sent the icy liquid over the sides of the container and onto the floor around Jake's shoes.

"Shit!" Jake cried out.

He leaped back and waited until the erupting liquid fell silent. He walked back to the cage and repeated the procedure, this time immersing Algernon's head into the second container. He quickly set up the equipment he would need to section tissue from Algernon's brain. After carefully removing thin slices of the rabbit's skull, Jake placed his gruesome samples beneath the microscope to search for answers. He turned on the microscope's ultraviolet light and was amazed by what he saw, glowing green bacteria, and lots of it. They had completely covered the cerebral cortex and had begun *replacing* the brain tissue.

"How the hell did they do that? They were only supposed to align themselves with the neural networks, not consume them!" Jake spluttered.

What was more disturbing to Jake was the fact that the bacteria had not only consumed parts of the neural tissue but for all intents and purposes *was* the animal's brain. The bacteria continued to survive and control the animal even after its apparent death. Icy fear gripped Jake.

"What have I done?" He suddenly remembered the other rabbit.

*Barney never received any immunosuppressant drugs. Could the bacteria have infected him from his encounter with Algernon?* He thought.

Langley' concern over human infection by the bacteria suddenly seemed very real. He raced over to the cage housing Barney. The rabbit seemed all right but then again so did Algernon.

*How long did the process take*? he asked himself.

Jake's mind was spinning, *How long had it been, a month*? Maybe, but he was having a hard time thinking clearly.

"Think Jake damn it, how long?"

He ran over to the lab computer. Frantically he searched his notes.

"There! About two weeks. That can't be right. Even ten days ago Algernon seemed fine," he reasoned.

Jake drew some blood from the site where Barney's leg was bitten off. He quickly made his way over to the scope and placed the blood on a slide. Jake's heart nearly stopped. Barney was infected with the glowing green bacteria. The professor went back to the biohazard bin and retrieved Barney's severed leg. Not wanting to waste time walking over to the dissection chamber, he dissected it right there and placed the leg beneath his microscope. Already he thought he could see bacteria silently aligning themselves with nerve tissue. He wondered if it was just his imagination, but clearly there *were* bacteria there and more were present than should be just an hour or so after infection.

"Oh my God!" Jake swallowed hard and fought the urge to panic.

"It can infect without immunosuppressant drugs! This stuff is not the Geobacter I engineered, it's…it's something different. How could this have happened?" Jake repeated over and over as he stood beside his microscope.

"If people were ever exposed to this I don't know what might…" Jake stopped in mid thought as his mind replayed the day's events.

"Christ, Ruben!"

Bill Santini and Marvin Freedmen weren't friends really, more like neighbors that lived at opposing ends of a very long street, but they did look out for one another. Bill would come to check on Marvin if the nights got very cold. He would make sure Marvin didn't stay in one place too long. If you overstayed your welcome on any sewer grate or manhole cover, the police would give you a hard time. They might even pick you up and drive you out of the city, only to dump you in the burbs where there was no place to keep warm.

*It would be nice if they'd take us to jail. A warm meal and a soft bed would be sweet.* A smile almost touched Bill's weather beaten face and swollen eyes as he made his way down 9th street towards Market.

Bill was a veteran of the first Gulf War and found it impossible to assimilate to civilian life after returning home. It wasn't the fact that he had lost most of his left arm during the war or his wife to another man. Simply put, he had seen too much. And when the Government refused to acknowledge the existence of Gulf War Syndrome it was too much to bear. Years of accumulated debt and alcoholism had taken their toll. Used up and spat out by the very world he sought to protect, he became bitter and homeless. However, he still sought meaning to his miserable existence. He had never given up his role as a protector, only now he protected other homeless people.

*I bet Marvin's been eatin' like a king down there. He owes me a drink and it's time to pay up,* his pace picked up considerably at the prospect of a little hooch.

He tucked his greasy black hair underneath his ball cap and hurried down the street.

Marvin was riding in a limousine with two beautiful women and listening to James Brown when a shot rang out. Pain coursed through his side as he heard a familiar voice shout his name.

"Marvin! Get up you lazy bum. How long have you been here?"

Marvin arose slowly from the sewer grate just as another shot rang out. Startled, he covered his head, but it was only a truck that had backfired.

Marvin growled at Bill, "What the hell'd you kick me for? You broke my damn ribs fool!"

Marvin had been on the streets for seventeen years and he still didn't know how he ended up there. Every now and then he would dream of his life before he was here, in this city, on this sewer grate, and homeless. Maybe that was just a dream. Memories that were more painful would try to intrude but they would always swirl and blend with the stench of the sewer until all he could think about was how to kill them away.

"I need some more medicine man," Marvin slurred.

"Hey you owe me! I ain't got nothin'. Slim pickins uptown brother. You been down here all day and what do you have to show for it? That's the last time I help your sorry ass out of a jam," Bill said half-heartedly.

"What you done did, other than break my ribs?! If you ain't gonna do nothin' but whine, then go on up out of here and leave me alone!" complained Marvin.

Bill chuckled to himself swinging his only arm as he walked down the street, looking back over his shoulder from time to time just to make sure Marvin had actually moved on. He really was fond of Marvin.

Ruben Stanley had to wait nearly an hour in the emergency room before a nurse finally saw him. His hand was hurting badly now. It was somewhat funny when he thought about it.

*Deranged rabbit attacks undergraduate at local University*, he imagined seeing the newspaper headlines and smiled.

But the pain was real. It had grown steadily worse since Algernon had bitten him.

*The bite is not that bad but it could use a few stitches, and that nurse, man is she hot. If I weren't dating Jennifer I'd... well I'd probably ask her out or...something*, Ruben's lack of experience with women was apparent even to himself as he analyzed his train of thought.

*She is hot though*, he concluded before trying to think of something else.

Heather came back into the room and asked Ruben a series of standard questions regarding his animal bite.

"You say this was a lab animal, Mr. Stanley? Was this animal vaccinated against rabies?"

"I don't know. I think so. I mean, yeah the University wouldn't buy any animal off the street. Yeah, I'm sure we have papers on them somewhere. I'll get someone to fax them..."

Heather interrupted Ruben's nervous attempt at sounding knowledgeable, "Mr. Stanley, I'm not trying to scare you. I just want to make sure that we cover all the bases here okay?"

Ruben smiled rather nervously and said, "Okay, but I'll still fax you those papers."

Heather tried to suppress a smile by wrinkling her mouth sideways and pretending she had an itch on her nose and said, "Good, you should."

Just then, Dr. Carl Wurling popped into the room.

"Hello, I'm Dr. Wurling. I hear you had a disagreement with a rabbit. I trust the rabbit is in worse shape than you are," he said while smiling.

Carl's humor and smile were infectious. Even his ex-wife thought so. It was probably because Carl meant just about everything he said or thought. He was genuine.

"Uh, well he...I mean he's kind of not doing too well. He was in a fight with another rabbit and I tried to separate them and that's when I was bitten," Ruben explained.

"You say the rabbit that bit you is not doing well?" asked Carl.

"Well Algernon, that's the one that bit me, he was torn up pretty badly by the other rabbit and I don't know if he's going to make it," Ruben replied.

"But the rabbit wasn't ill before the fight?"

"No he was fine."

Carl fixed his gaze on Ruben for a long moment, smiling all the while.

"Well if your rabbit was okay then we have nothing to be concerned about. We are going to give you a tetanus shot and some antibiotics to be on the safe side. Take some Tylenol for the pain and don't get between any more rabbits having a squabble alright?"

"Okay," Ruben replied sheepishly.

It was four o'clock in the morning and the professor still hadn't been able to get in touch with Ruben. He left messages on Ruben and Jennifer's voicemail but hadn't been able to speak with anyone. He had thoroughly disinfected the lab and placed Barney in an isolation chamber thinking the rabbit may hold the key to understanding what he'd witnessed earlier in the day. But right now he wanted to talk with Ruben to make sure he was alright. Everything that had happened sounded like the beginning of a bad zombie movie.

Jake stopped in mid thought and declared, "I have to get some sleep. Now I'm delirious. If I talk with anyone right now I'll probably sound insane and get locked up in the loony bin…zombies," Jake shook his head.

"I need a drink."

Jake Northrop left the lab and drove to his very modest, single bedroom apartment a few miles from the University.

Jake didn't drink heavily very often but when he did it was bad. Jake was worried that he'd made a terrible mistake using *Geobacter*. Still, he couldn't understand for the life of him what went wrong.

"Geobacter… zombies," he slurred.

"Zombacter, ZOMBACTER!" He smiled as he continued saying the word over and over again.

He thought it rolled off his tongue rather eloquently even if he was too drunk to enunciate it properly.

"It worked though, by God! They replicated neural networks swimmingly well! Bio-computer my ASS! Freakin' zombie rabbit's what I created!" Jake shouted at his whiskey bottle as he stood waving it in the air.

With all the lights out, he paced back and forth across his eighth floor- apartment overlooking Center City and the Schuylkill River. The lights of a passing car shined through the blinds and caught his attention. He stumbled over to the window, parted the blinds with his fingers and saw people down below on their way to and from a tavern and thought…

*Humans with their problems...their own lives...oblivious to me...to what I've created...what I may've done.*

Taking another big gulp of whiskey he imagined the drunken people he saw staggering about were actually zombies spreading his deadly plague though the city. Even though the thought was repellent, it somehow intrigued him. He raised his arms in the manner of the living dead and moaned, "Wooooo!"

He began laughing silently, holding his side as wave after wave of uncontrollable mirth washed over him. It was the absurdity of it all. He was a scientist not given to flights of self-indulgent fantasy like this. It must be the alcohol and the stress. He'd never been a fan of horror movies but once again he had the feeling this was how they all began.

Then a sobering thought came to him, *the bacteria align themselves with neural networks because they can sense bioelectricity. A large EMF pulse should disrupt their ability to communicate and mimic host brain activity.*

If, of course, he ever had the need to stop a zombie, that might come in handy. Jake knew it was the alcohol talking. Still, he allowed his mind to wander for the time being. Jake considered the results of *Zombacter* spreading into the human population.

"Christ it might be as bad as HIV. With a two-week incubation period, people could carry it half way around the globe not knowing they were infected," he slurred while dropping his head to his chest.

Jake fell against the wall next to the window and slid down to the floor. Now facing his darkened room, he continued his ruminations. *But it would take an enormous number of people infected initially to spread the disease and that isn't likely. How would we know who was infected? How would the symptoms manifest*?

He remembered how the genetically altered bacteria had modified the rabbit's behavior.

"Bite to infect, continuation of the species," Jake's drunken mind whirled as he spoke to himself.

*Is this how people would spread it, the same way as the rabbit, by biting someone? I wonder if Algernon was dead when he bit Barney. What a strange thought*, Jake mused.

At that moment, Jake wished that he had recorded every second of the experiment so he could witness the stages of the transformation. Still he had a hard time coming to grips with bacteria that seemed to create zombie rabbits. The day's events pursued him relentlessly into unconsciousness.

# GET RID OF THEM

**October 23**
**Potterfield Science Building:**

Langley' face was purple as he stood inside the pungent laboratory poking his finger into Jake's chest.

"My daughter was around those goddamn rabbits! You told me that people couldn't get infected by that stuff!"

"I don't think they can," Jake protested.

"You don't think they can? That's not what I heard on my daughter's voicemail. You sounded worried as hell!"

"I was drunk!"

"That's your problem! I don't want to know any more about it just get some help!" Langley yelled.

"I never said people could be infected. I just wanted the kids to be aware that the rabbits had a bad reaction to their treatments and to stay away from them until I could figure out what went wrong."

"I'd say they didn't react well. One of them is dead!" Langley fired back sarcastically.

"I had to put that one down because of his injuries, not because he was sick. I already explained that to you."

"What about Ruben?"

"Jennifer told me he saw a doctor yesterday and he's fine. They gave him some antibiotics as a precaution but there's nothing to worry about," said Jake reassuringly.

Langley stormed toward the animal cages and pointed at them.

"I want this…all this…gone…both rabbits and that crap you stuck 'em with!" he demanded.

"What? You can't expect me to throw my research down the drain! I'm too close! I need to find out what went wrong!" protested Jake.

"Maybe you don't hear so well Jake. I said get rid of it!" yelled Langley.

"You can't be serious! I'm six months away from the damn bio-computer! Ron, I swear to you I'm on the right track! Just give me a few days I…"

"As soon as you're the boss around here then you can do whatever the hell you want! But I'm telling you to go back to the starting board with this one and if you don't take care of this I'll come down here and do it myself!"

"What the hell's wrong with you? Nanotech isn't going to wait for us to come up with an alternative! There is no alternative! This is the only thing that has the slightest chance of working and now you want me to dump it in the toilet! You're crazy!"

"You heard what I said Professor Northrop," Langley said ominously as he left the lab and slammed the door behind him.

Jake knew that Langley was already planning to destroy the rabbits. It was a typical knee-jerk reaction he'd seen before, people who were scared of something because they didn't understand it. Those were dangerous people.

Jake understood the only way he was going to save his research was by archiving samples of live and dead rabbit tissue. Algernon's remains were already preserved in a cryogenic state so all that remained was to preserve samples of Barney's tissue. Barney still seemed healthy so Jake quickly took samples of the rabbit's tissues for future analyses.

Jake reassuringly said to the one-legged rabbit, "I'm sorry old buddy but I'm going to have to put you down. This won't hurt a bit."

Jake was saddened by what he had to do but he knew it was the only way to outwit Langley. Jake administered the lethal cocktail that would forever put the rabbit to sleep. The rabbit kicked and quivered for only a few seconds before going limp. The professor placed Barney in a biohazard bag and slipped it into another cryogenic cylinder for storage.

Blaine was on his way down to Jake's lab when he bumped into Ronald Langley.

"Sorry Dr. Langley I didn't see you," apologized Blaine.

"Blaine, I want you to get rid of those rabbits down in Dr. Northrop's lab."

"Isn't he still using them?"

"He's finished. Now get rid of them. Do you understand me? *Today* Blaine!" exclaimed Langley while jabbing his finger into Blaine's chest.

"Yes sir, Dr. Langley. I'll get right on it." Blaine replied.

Satisfied, Langley stomped off down the hall.

"*Man, Langley seemed really pissed. I hope he's not mad at me for something I really need this job*," thought Blaine.

Jake was leaving as Blaine approached the door to the lab.

"Blaine, I have to run a few errands but I'll be back later this afternoon. Don't go near the lab animals when you're cleaning up and don't touch the computer. I'm working on something important and it's compiling right now. It should be finished by the time I get back."

"No problem. Hey, is Rubes coming in today? I got one of his books he let me borrow," Blaine said while smiling.

"Rubes? Ah, you mean Ruben. I didn't know who you were talking about at first."

"I like to call him Rubes, huh-huh. He hates it when I call him that, huh-huh." Blaine replied in a perfect imitation of Butthead from the 1990's T.V. show *Beavis and Butthead*, only he wasn't trying to imitate Butthead. He naturally sounded like a stoned surfer.

"Well then why do it?"

"Uh, I don't know. It's just kinda funny you know, huh-huh."

"Right… well I'm sure he'll be here later. Just leave it on my desk in the lab."

Jake walked down the hall shaking his head. Blaine watched him until he disappeared around the corner.

"See you brau."

Blaine walked into the lab and scanned the area for the rabbit cages. They were both empty. The other lab animals were busily going about their normal routines and Blaine paid them no attention. He knew he had to find those rabbits. Although Blaine wasn't the sharpest tool in the shed, he understood that more was at risk than his internship. His father had told him as much.

*One more screw-up Blaine and so help me God; you can wash cars for the rest of your life! I will not support your partying lifestyle any longer! You got me son?*

"Yeah, I got ya dad," Blaine said to himself. He searched all over the room before something shining under the fume hood caught his attention. Blaine lifted the hood and hefted one of the gleaming canisters into the air. He unscrewed the lid and could see part of a biohazard bag peeking out of the liquid nitrogen.

"There you are," said Blaine, rather pleased at his discovery.

*This will be easier than I thought. I'll just throw 'em in a bag and carry 'em to the dump like a couple of frozen chickens,* Blaine chuckled.

The other canister held a more gruesome payload. Blaine opened it, fished out Algernon's remains, and plopped them unceremoniously into the garbage bag.

"Damn man! What was the professor doin' with this rabbit? I guess he didn't like you little dude!" Blaine said to the frozen rabbit head.

With his frozen cargo in a black plastic trash bag, he headed outside to the dumpster. Blaine was annoyed when he discovered it had a lock on it.

"Man I have to carry these things around in my car!" he whined.

He shoved the plastic bag into his trunk and drove around campus searching for a dumpster. A few minutes later hunger re-routed his plans. He decided to drive over to Terminal Market to get a bite to eat; there he could dump the carcasses. Blaine found the perfect location in an alley near Arch Street and 8$^{th}$. He lifted the lid of the dumpster and threw in the garbage bag. The frozen corpses made a loud metallic banging noise as they hit the bottom of the empty refuse container. The noise startled Blaine and he looked around to see if anyone had noticed. He hurried inside the market for some of Philly's best hot and spicy Thai.

# FRANK

**November 10**
**New Jersey Landfill:**

Frank was in a wonderful mood. The sun shone down brightly on his deep brown face for the first time in weeks. He smiled up at the sky with his eyes closed and breathed in the morning air. Frank loved his job.

"Come on Frank! Help us get this shit heap unloaded will ya!" yelled Johnny Sampson, Frank's friend and coworker.

Frank's smile never left his face as he walked across the landfill to help guide the trucks attempting to maneuver in and around the landfill so they could dump their pungent cargo.

"I'm coming. Wouldn't wanna keep the city waitin, no sir unh uh."

At lunchtime, Frank walked around poking through the trash to see what treasures he could find. The smells of diesel fuel and garbage mixed with the scents of the fresh air and the sea. He soon tired of searching through the trash and turned his attention to more important matters. Frank wandered around for quite a while looking for the family of foxes that lived at the landfill. He finally spotted the red tail of a fox and began walking toward it. He wasn't even halfway there when he realized something was wrong. Concerned, he jogged over to the fox and was saddened by what he saw.

"Oh man, not the momma. What happened to you? Where are your babies little momma? Oh no, without their momma them babies are gonna starve," Frank said, worriedly.

The female red fox was dead, more to the point she had been torn apart. Frank continued walking in an ever-widening circle.

Pieces of fur were everywhere. Frank picked up a bright white piece with the jaws of his trash poker.

*It's a rabbit's leg,* Frank thought.

He continued searching until his eyes found what he was looking for, well not really. The baby foxes were also dead and mutilated.

"Man what did this? What did this to my little family?" Frank asked, nearly in tears.

He reached out with his metal poker to turn a young fox over when, from out of nowhere, he was attacked.

"Ahhggg!!! Get off uh me! Damn, my hand! Son of a bitch! You done it now!" Frank yelled as he knocked the male fox to the ground.

He stepped on its neck with his boot but was careful not to kill it.

"Damn little man, you messed up my hand! Why did you go and do a thing like that for huh? I didn't hurt you! Man, what's wrong with you? Aw shit, you got rabies don't you? Damn! Now I have to get all those shots! Damn! Johnny! Johnny! I need a hand! Come here man! I need some help here! Bring a box or something!"

Frank King and Johnny Sampson put the struggling fox in a live trap that had not been used since Frank started getting close to the family of animals earlier this year. Frank wrapped his hand in paper towels and his jacket as they made their way back toward the truck.

Johnny was nagging Frank, "Didn't I tell you to leave those things alone Frank? I said if you keep messin' around with wild animals, one day you're gonna get bit didn't I?"

Frank barked back, "Shut up man! Just shut up! My hand's hurtin' bad! Man, he messed it up! I can't move my fingers! It's bleedin real bad. You gotta hurry!"

Johnny tried to reassure Frank, "You're gonna be alright Frank. Don't worry. I know it looks bad but I've seen a lot worse than that and they came out just fine."

Johnny drove Frank to the E.R. and lectured him some more about wild animal behavior. Frank turned on the radio to drown him out.

Frank's co-worker walked him into the emergency room and helped him sign in.

"Now look Frank, you're gonna be just fine. I'm gonna take that fox over to the vet to get him tested for rabies so maybe you won't have to get those shots huh? Then I'm coming back to check on you all right? I won't be gone long; traffic was light on the way up."

"Johnny, call my wife and tell her I'm gonna be late, okay?" pleaded Frank.

"You got it pal," Johnny said as he slapped Frank on the back.

Jill Sorenson was a great veterinarian. Dr. Sorenson had recently bought out her partner's half of the small animal clinic they both ran in Philadelphia. At thirty-eight years old, Jill had already accomplished more than most of her peers back in college. She was the primary author on numerous publications including her Opus, which was published in a prestigious journal, and she owned her own home. Although she was not wealthy by her colleagues' standards, she led a comfortable life while pursuing her dreams. She was well respected among the veterinary community and was well liked by her clients and *most* of her patients.

Dr. Sorenson was enjoying a fine career indeed. She had very little to complain about. She lived a nearly picture-perfect existence with only one exception, and the medical I.D. bracelet she always wore was testimony to that. Jill had a congenital heart defect, a life-threatening one. She had to wear a pacemaker to ensure that her heart would beat regularly and continuously. Despite appearing a bit frail, the blonde-haired, blue-eyed Dr. Sorenson was still a very pretty woman.

Jill was getting ready to call it an early day when a man burst through the door with a live trap containing a snarling fox.

"What do you have there? Is that a fox?" Jill asked.

"Lady, this fox bit my friend down at the landfill and we need to get it tested for rabies. Can you do that for us?" asked Johnny.

"Well you're in luck. I'm actually one of the few pet clinics around here that'll send samples to the state veterinary diagnostic lab for testing. We won't know the results for a couple weeks. But…I can also use a relatively new test that'll give us results today but we'll still need to check them against the state tests to be sure. Let me have a look."

The fox suddenly stopped snarling and lay down on the bottom of the cage.

"Yeah he is acting weird. You had better leave him here. I'll take care of it. Give me a number where you can be reached."

Johnny wrote the number down on the back of a business card and handed it to Jill.

"Look, I'm going back over to the hospital to check on my pal."

"I'll let you know something as soon as I have the results."

"Great. Thanks Doc." And with that, Johnny left for the hospital.

Jill thought to herself, *Looks like rabies all right…but he seems so docile now.*

As Dr. Sorenson approached the cage, the fox began to quiver and moved to the far corner of the cage. His eyes darted around wildly but became fixed on Jill when she stepped closer to the cage. The fox was desperately searching for a way out.

"This is not at all like an animal with rabies. A rabid fox wouldn't fear me," she said aloud.

"I hate to do this to you fellow but there's only one way find out."

Jill went to the back to get the dart gun. When she came back the fox was lying flat on his side with his tongue hanging out the side of his mouth.

"What in the hell? Now that is odd."

She approached the cage cautiously and pointed the dart gun at the apparently unconscious fox. Just to be sure, she pulled the trigger and the gun made a loud pop. The fox did not flinch. Jill left the animal and went to prepare her work area.

She needed only a small sample of saliva for the faster field version of the test but to be sure, she would have to excise the brain and send tissue samples in to the health department. She put on her thick black gloves and opened the cage where the fox lay dead. She took her syringe, removed saliva, and then swabbed the animal's mouth with a large Q-tip. As she was finishing the fox sprang to its feet and snapped at Jill.

"Oh shit!" she screamed and slammed the cage door on the fox until it pulled its head back inside.

*I know I just popped him with enough stuff to take down a horse! I've never seen an animal do that before. Jesus that crap must be out of date. I really need to check that stock in the morning. He almost got me,* Jill thought.

Again, the fox lay silent on the bottom of the cage but this time he most certainly did not seem afraid. In fact, he sat motionless as if he were sizing her up.

Jill's heart was still pounding as she began the analyses of the fox spittle. Her pacemaker was doing its job. It was then she felt a burning sensation like a paper cut and the inside of her glove felt wet. Jill tore her glove off to examine her hand. It was a tiny scratch with no blood to speak of. The wetness in her glove was perspiration. She wondered if the scratch had been there all along. She turned the glove over in her hand to look for any sort of puncture or tear but couldn't find any. Then she stretched the edge of the glove that would have been in contact with the side of her hand and there it was; a tiny cut in the glove less than a centimeter long. She stared at it for a moment and then looked back at the cage.

*There are so many sharp edges. I probably just caught it on the cage when I jerked my hand out of his reach*, she thought.

She had to gas the fox to put it down and even then, it continued to writhe around until she removed the brain. Normally a vet would just sever the animal's head and send the whole kit and caboodle in for testing but Jill had the facilities to do a postmortem brain extraction. This way she could collect samples and send only the tissues needed for the test and save money on the brain extraction done by the state.

Dr. Sorenson severed the animal's head at the base of the neck exposing the entryway into the skull, the foramen magnum. She inserted a spoon-shaped instrument into the hole and scooped out a walnut-sized portion of the cerebellum. She placed her cargo into tiny vials that sat nestled in a heavy-duty Styrofoam carton. Once she packaged them for the more reliable state lab test, she concentrated on the faster and less expensive saliva test she could conduct.

Jill placed the fox saliva onto a sterile concave glass slide filled with microscopic blue-latex beads sensitized with rabies immunoglobulin. She gently mixed the saliva with the latex and watched for the telltale signs of agglutination. If the latex clumped together then the test would be positive for rabies.

Dr. Sorenson watched the little puddle of latex and spittle intently as she gently swirled the mixture. It took less than fifteen minutes before the test was complete. Strangely, it came back negative for rabies. Although she was very relieved, something still bothered her about the animal's odd behavior. She couldn't be absolutely certain that it wasn't rabies until the state tests came back, but she felt confident enough that it wasn't the virus and she called the man who brought the fox in to give him the results.

"I don't know what was wrong with that animal but it wasn't rabies."

"Frank's gonna be okay then?" Johnny asked.

"Well he won't come down with rabies if that's what you mean."

"Thank you for everything Doc."

"Don't mention it," Sorenson concluded before hanging up the phone.

Her clinic had a crematorium and Jill disposed of the fox that same evening. It had been a very strange afternoon indeed.

Frank's hand required twenty-two stitches to close the wound left by the fox. He would need to undergo another surgery to restore movement in his pinky and ring fingers. He still felt bad about the fox. He hadn't known that an animal must be euthanized before it could be definitively determined rabies-free.

"Hey, I can still use you down at the site. Besides, you're worth two men even if you only have one hand!" Johnny complimented Frank.

"Thanks but I think the wife is gonna be needin' me around the house. Johnny, I ain't lying. I've never felt pain like I felt today. I don't know what it is but I feel like I've been shot and stabbed at the same time, all from this little bite."

"I wouldn't call that a little bite Frank. He took a quarter of your hand there buddy. Look, get some rest and give me a call when you get up. Just tell me how long you think you're gonna need okay?"

"Alright man. I think I'm gonna be taking all my vacation though…Grand Canyon…me and the wife always wanted to go there."

"Hey, take as long as you need. You just get better alright? And send me some pictures."

**November 14**
***No Tell Motel*, Arizona:**

Frank and his wife were in a small, shabby motel about an hour's drive from the Grand Canyon. Their room smelled of cigarette-smoke and Lysol and had a color-scheme straight out of the seventies. On any other day Frank never would've considered staying at this motel but he was just too sick to continue. Besides, it was Frank's idea to drive across the United States even though he wasn't feeling well and they really didn't have the money for a vacation. Frank knew he couldn't let another day go by without doing some of the things he and his wife had always dreamed about. It was the loss of his surrogate fox-family that made him decide to spend what little money they did have.

Frank started feeling crummy back in Jersey the day before they left. He knew there was something going around so he thought nothing of it. After all, Frank was a tough man. He wasn't going to let something like a cold stop him and his family from enjoying a well-deserved vacation. But for Frank, a common cold soon became a burning fever with nausea that wouldn't go away. His ears were ringing so loudly he couldn't concentrate on anything for more than a few minutes at a time. Frank went downhill from there.

He began retching into the toilet on and off five hours earlier. His wife Delores was very worried about him. She had never seen her husband in such a terrible state and thought that his sickness might be related to the nasty bite on his hand. Frank was a big, strong man that rarely got sick and now he could barely drag himself into the bathroom to vomit.

"Frank, let me take you to the hospital baby. You can barely stand on your own."

"I'm not goin' to no hospital! I already told you that! We're on vacation and I'm not spendin' it there! I'll be fine in the mornin'," Frank argued as he staggered back toward the bed.

"It's just a stomach flu, that's all."

"Yeah, you're gonna be alright in the morning, uh huh! Were gonna be stuck in this motel for most our vacation! Let's go to the doctor and get you something for this. Maybe you'll be able to get *some* kinda sleep," Delores pleaded.

"Leave me alone woman! I got enough rollin' roun' in my head without you addin' to it!"

"Fine then, puke your guts out! See if I care! Drag me across the country for *this!* See if I go anywhere else with you! Grumpy ole bastard!"

And with that, Delores crawled into the other twin bed, turned her back to Frank and covered her ears with pillows.

This really wasn't like him at all. Frank loved his wife and normally didn't snap at her like this. He tried to apologize to Delores but it was no use. She wouldn't have it. He felt terrible about the whole thing but was too sick to do much about it. Frank's head kept spinning as he lay on his back in bed. He couldn't sleep. It was only a matter of time before he would need to run to the bathroom again.

Later that night Delores awoke from a shallow sleep. She was struck by the fact that for the first time this evening it was quiet. The sounds of Frank's violent retching were gone. Delores turned her head and looked over at the other twin bed, noticing her husband wasn't in it. She sat up and looked toward the darkened bathroom doorway.

Squinting into the inky blackness Delores thought, *"Frank didn't turn the light on this time."*

Instinctively she felt that something was seriously wrong with her husband. Delores hopped out of bed and walked over to the bathroom. Dim, peach-colored street light spilled into the small motel room between the yellowing curtains. She thought she could see movement inside the bathroom.

"Frank?" She turned the light on and gasped when she saw Frank lying on his side.

"Frank, oh my God!"

Blood was spattered on the floor and the inside of the toilet bowl. His eyes and mouth were open and his face was covered with vomit. His pants were down to his ankles and coated with excrement and blood. With a loud pop, the single, dirty light-bulb suddenly blew-out leaving Delores in the dark.

"Oh my God Frank, get up!" Delores shouted frantically.

She reached over to try to find Frank. Her hand found only a thick, slippery substance that could only be one of a few things and the thought of any of them made her stomach churn. As her eyes grew accustomed to the darkness, she thought she could see a dim form moving toward her.

"Frank?" she called out nervously.

Something cold touched her outstretched hand.

"Frank? You're freezing are you…Arrrggggghhh!" Screamed Delores.

Delores drew back what was left of her hand and held it in front of her face. She couldn't see well in the poor light but jets of warm blood spurted into her eyes and open mouth. She was now missing the last three fingers of her right hand just below the knuckles. Delores fell backward and scrambled out of the bathroom, crying and groaning in agony. Something else was squirming along after her.

"Help me! Oh God help me!"

She got to her feet and was able to use the feeble streetlight that made it past the gauntlet of cigarette smoke yellowed tapestries to find the door but her bloody hand kept slipping around the doorknob.

"Please, please, please!" she cried.

Mercifully, the tarnished knob turned and the door swung open. Delores ran out into the parking lot screaming for help. It took five full minutes of screaming and banging on doors before someone finally came out to see what was going on. All the while Frank was slowly moving out into the parking lot. He was on his belly with his soiled pants still around his ankles, searching for something or someone. Delores stopped her frantic cries for help once or twice, mesmerized and totally confused by what she was witnessing. Frank barely held his head off the ground and seemed to be using every muscle in his body in an undulating fashion. His grotesque and unnatural movements resembled those of a newborn, only they were more worm-like and fluid. He made no noise that Delores could hear.

Between her cries for help, she would half-sob and half-scream, "Frank why are you doing this?"

The man that came to Delores's rescue was just as confused as she was by the surreal scene playing out before them. He ushered Delores King into his motel room and called 911.

"911, what is your emergency?"

"There's an injured lady here. A man bit some of her fingers off. She's bleeding really badly and I think she's in shock."

"Sir, what is your name?"

"Don… Donny Drescoe."

"Donny you said someone's injured and they're bleeding?"

"Yes! Her hand's all messed up. The guy that did it is still crawling around in the damn parking lot!"

"I have your location as the Grand Canyon Inn, Junction 180 & N. Highway 64, Williams, Arizona. Is this correct?"

"No but its close, that's about two miles West of here. We're just off of the highway. I'm at the *No Tell Motel*."

"Donny, try to stay calm, help is on the way. Are you safe? Are you injured?"

"Yeah I'm safe but I'm scared shitless! I don't know what's going on here."

"Is the injured person there with you now?"

"Yeah, she's lying on the floor. She's bleeding all over the place. How long will it take you guys to get here?"

"It will be about thirty minutes. I need you to apply First-Aid to the injured person."

"What! Uh-uhh! No way José! I'm not touching her! That's not my responsibility! I did my part. Get your asses over here and take care of this! I'm not touching her! That fellow out in the parking lot is in bad shape. He looks really sick and I don't want whatever he has."

"Sir, I just need you to apply direct pressure to the wound until help arrives."

"You can apply direct pressure to my ass cheek lady! I'M NOT TOUCHING HER!"

"Do you have any towels that could be used to absorb the blood?"

"Yeah maybe."

"Is the victim conscious?"

"I think so…yeah she's looking at me now."

"Give her the towels and tell her to apply direct pressure to the wound to stop the bleeding."

Donny looked over at Delores while holding the phone away from his mouth and said rather inconsiderately, "Hey they said you should put this towel on the wound and apply pressure until help arrives okay."

Delores stared blankly at the man and nodded.

"Yeah I think she's listening. She's holding the towel on her hand now."

"Donny that's great. You've done a good thing tonight. Thank you."

"Hey uh, just doing my part you know," Donny said with a self-absorbed grin.

The paramedics, Burt Townsend and Jeffrey Moore, arrived along with the sheriff Roy Clay and his deputy Joy Ferguson a short time later. The sheriff was surprised to see Frank slowly clawing at the motel door where Donny and Delores were holed up.

"You, hold it right there! Hey buddy, you listening to me?"

Frank didn't respond or cease his futile efforts to get into the motel room. The sheriff gauged the situation and decided he had little to fear from this man. The 6'- tall, 230 lb sheriff put his knee in the center of Frank's back and pulled out his handcuffs.

"Okay mister, I'm gonna handcuff you now so just take it easy, alright?"

Frank began to turn towards the sheriff during the handcuffing process and Roy started yelling at him with a deep and booming voice.

"Stay still damn it or I'll have to use force!"

Roy was trying to keep Frank's massive arms together behind his back but Frank kept them pulling away from him. To make matters worse, biting flies were harassing the sheriff as he attempted to subdue Frank.

"Joy! Give me a hand here! This son of a bitch is strong as an ox!"

But a cloud of dust was now partially obscuring the two struggling men from outside observers. Knowing the sheriff needed more strength than Joy could give, she ran back to the car to get a non-lethal weapon.

"Where the hell are you going? Didn't you hear me?" Roy shouted over his shoulder at Joy.

Once again, Frank thwarted Roy's attempts to keep his arms behind his back. This time the heavily muscled sheriff held on tightly to Frank's right arm as he swung it back in front of his head. Frank swiftly turned his head and sank his teeth into Roy's bicep. Frank slowly worked his teeth from side to side, shearing off a mouth-sized portion of Roy's arm.

"Arghhhhhhh!" Roy squeezed his blue eyes shut and screamed as the pain shot through his arm.

"Get away from him Roy!" Joy screamed as she pointed a gun at Frank.

Roy rolled off to the side clutching his bleeding arm. With a loud pop, Joy fired her weapon. Two long wires were now attaching Frank's back to Joy's Taser gun. Frank convulsed briefly and then started worming his way toward Joy. She shocked him again with the same result. Suddenly, another shot rang out from behind Joy causing her to jump. She spun around to see Burt holding another Taser. With renewed vigor, Joy faced Frank again and pulled the trigger. Frank was receiving the full brunt of two Tasers. After being shocked repeatedly, he finally stopped his advance.

"Jesus what in the hell is he on!?" the sheriff said aloud, grimacing in pain. "I've never seen anything like this. Cuff that asshole before he wakes up!"

"Oh man we've gotta get you to the hospital Roy! He did a number on your arm," Joy said while kneeling beside the sheriff.

"You think? Why the hell didn't you help me back there? With your body weight and mine we could've pinned him and he wouldn't have taken a chunk out of my arm!"

"Come on sheriff! He was throwing you around like a rag doll. We would've both gotten hurt. As soon as I saw that you were in trouble I ran back to the patrol car to get the Taser."

Roy saw the logic in her statement and decided it was wise not to argue with her. She was very intelligent and he had grown to like the way she argued with him. It also didn't hurt that she was easy on the eyes.

"Hey you're hurt. What happened to your hand? You need to get Jeffrey to look at that," Roy said worriedly.

"He just scratched me a little while I was cuffing him. I'll live. You're the one that needs a doctor."

The sheriff looked over at Burt who was playing quick draw with the Taser gun.

"Who gave Burt a Taser anyway?"

Burt smiled and said, "We've had this in the ambulance for years and no one's used it until now. It gets serviced regularly along with the fire extinguisher. I figured you guys needed a hand."

"Great," Roy said while shaking his head.

Jeffrey administered first aid to the sheriff and told him he would probably need surgery where he'd been bitten. Roy remained stoic throughout the entire ordeal.

Burt and Jeffrey loaded Delores into the ambulance and told Joy she'd have to take the assailant to the hospital in the sheriff's car. The sheriff complained bitterly that he would have to share the same vehicle with the smelly man that bit him.

The ambulance was preparing for departure when the sheriff shouted, "Hey I need to talk to her!"

"You can talk to her at the hospital sheriff. She's not in any shape to talk at the moment. She's in shock," replied Burt solemnly.

"Good enough. I'll see you in a little while Burt."

The long trip to the hospital in Flagstaff was relatively uneventful and yet annoying to Joy. Frank had regained consciousness and was biting at the cage separating him from the law enforcement officers while Roy continuously yelled at him to stop. Joy was grateful when she saw the hospital signs appearing by the roadside.

"Alright, this is it sheriff. Let's get you stitched-up and get this fellow some help."

"What he needs is a bullet in the head!"

"Enough Roy! Let's just get someone to help us with this guy and call it a night. I can file the paper work but you need to get some rest."

A burly orderly helped drag Frank into the hospital where he was handcuffed to a chair. All the while Frank kept attempting to bite anyone within reach.

Roy was finally able to talk to Delores but what she said just didn't add up. She painted a picture of her husband Frank as a sensitive, caring man that would no sooner harm a fly than another person.

*Why the hell did he do this to the woman he loved?* Roy thought.

Delores had only one explanation. She said a rabid fox bit Frank a few days ago and that he became ill on their vacation. Roy asked how she knew this and Delores recounted Frank's story of the fox family and how the vet claimed the fox didn't have rabies. Delores was sure the vet had made a mistake. Delores seemed very convincing but the sheriff had seen ordinary people do some horrible things because of drugs. Roy immediately sent for Frank's medical records and criminal history. Roy felt sure that Delores was in denial about Frank. He tried to ask her if Frank had been using drugs and that just made her furious with the sheriff.

She screamed at Roy, "You don't know anything about us! Just because we're black you have to make this about drugs! Just mind your own damn business!"

"Time will tell," Roy said to Delores on the way out.

The physician on duty came into the room where Roy and Joy were standing guard over their prisoner.

"What do we have here sheriff?" he said while looking back and forth between Frank and Roy. The young doctor was clearly irritated at seeing a visibly ill patient in handcuffs.

"Look Doc I know what you're thinking but this man has attacked two people, myself included." Roy held his arm up to illustrate his point.

"Can we agree that his pants need to be around his waist and not his ankles?" The doctor said contemptuously.

"I don't care where his pants are and I don't think he does either! I just want to know what's wrong with him and if I need to get rabies shots or something!"

The doctor shook his head and proceeded toward his patient. Frank's chin was resting on his chest and he hadn't moved in half an hour.

Without looking back at Roy the doctor said, "I think your dangerous prisoner is dead."

"I don't think…"

"No, I don't guess you people are trained to think!" The doctor spat his words, cutting Roy off in mid sentence.

"Doc you don't understand."

"Let's get something straight here! This is my patient and I'll decide how he is to be handled! Get those handcuff's off of him now!" venom dripping off every word the doctor spoke.

"Fine, don't say I didn't warn you," Roy said clearly and ominously. "Joy, get that door will you. Get ready okay. You know what he's capable of."

Joy closed the door and stood watching as Roy unshackled Frank from the chair.

"There, are you happy now?" Roy said with sarcasm.

"I want you to uncuff his hands sheriff."

"Absolutely not! It took three people and two stun guns to subdue this creep!"

The doctor rounded on Roy and pointed toward Frank, "So that's how you killed him. How many times did you shock him?"

"You are out of line Doc. I've had about enough of your attitude."

"Look at this man! He isn't breathing. He's dead! As far as I can tell, the only threat in this room is standing in front of me! Get those handcuff's off him before I press charges against you and your deputy!"

"You are some piece of work. Just because you've got a degree you think you can look down your nose at everybody else," Roy said while squinting down at the doctor.

Looking back at Joy the sheriff nodded and said, "Joy, you heard everything right? You heard me warn him right?"

Joy nodded back and said, "Roy, just do as he said. I wanna get some sleep before my shift starts again."

Shaking his head Roy walked behind Frank's chair and reluctantly removed the handcuffs. He quickly stepped back and drew his gun.

"Put that away sheriff! You might accidentally shoot someone."

"If I shoot anyone it's not gonna be an accident Doc."

The doctor put his hand on Frank's neck, shook his head and then gently raised Frank's head. The doctor lifted Frank's eyelid revealing a milky, dead stare. Shaking his head again, he shined his penlight into Frank's eye.

"Dead as a doornail, this doesn't look good for either of you," he said while clicking his tongue.

"Are you sure? This is the way he looked earlier and he still managed this," again, Roy held his arm up for effect.

The doctor spoke to Roy as one would a child, slowly and carefully.

"Subtle as the signs of life may be, say a warm body, a pulse, a heartbeat, pupils that aren't fixed and dilated, I would expect that even you could tell if someone were alive or dead."

"Can you tell me then, what was wrong with him? Do I need to be worried about this," Roy held his arm up again and pointed to the wound.

"Are you so dim-witted that you are unable to grasp the implications of what I'm telling you? You and your deputy killed a man! From everything I've seen and from your own admission, you shocked him to death!"

"Now wait just a minute. He was alive on the way over here."

"Yeah, he kept biting at the cage and Roy was yelling at him. They were both driving me crazy. Roy is telling you the truth. He was alive on the way over and was even trying to get at the orderly."

"I think you're both lying. This man has been dead for hours. You don't look like that after half an hour!"

Roy's fists clenched involuntarily. "You little turd!" he said, stomping toward the doctor.

"Roy don't! He's not worth it! Let it go! We know what we saw."

"Have it your way Doc. You do what you have to do. Me and my deputy are going home."

Roy pointed his finger at the doctor's chest and added, "Oh, and I want you to test that son of a bitch for rabies. His wife said he got bit by a rabid animal and that's why he was attacking people. I'll consider it a crime if you don't. You get my drift son?"

"Are you threatening me sheriff?"

Roy turned his back toward the arrogant doctor and began walking away.

"No sir, that's a promise," he said matter-of-factly.

Roy and his deputy left the hospital and began their trip back to the station. There was paperwork to file and although Joy wasn't looking forward to it, she'd promised to take care of it. Joy was proud of the way the sheriff had handled himself tonight. He stood up to that doctor and wasn't sucked into a physical altercation with him. She could see settling down with someone like Roy Clay. If only he would see her the same way.

The young doctor was examining Frank for signs of police brutality when Frank twitched. It was just the smallest of twitches but the doctor saw it.

He reasoned to himself, *It's a little late for muscles twitches but I guess it's not unheard of.*

Satisfied, the doctor continued looking Frank over. There were so many injuries to document.

Outside the room where Frank was being examined, the orderly, who had assisted in bringing Frank in, was getting supplies ready on a cart. He was startled when screams erupted from the examination room.

# HYSTERIA

**November 28**
**Potterfield Science Building:**

"Where's Ruben? He hasn't been in for days and he hasn't called either." Dr. Northrop inquired.

"Oh he's in Houston, Texas visiting his sick grandmother. He had to leave right away. I was supposed to tell you guys but I kinda forgot," Jennifer explained. "Yeah, he called me yesterday to tell me she wasn't doing very well and he didn't know when he'd be back."

Jake stared at Jennifer for quite some time before grunting, "Uh huh" and dismissing his paranoia.

Jennifer felt uneasy lying for Ruben but she was afraid that he would lose his job if they thought he was just skipping work. She was worried about him too. The last time she had heard from Ruben he was sick. He told her it was probably the flu and he didn't want her to catch it. She didn't want to get sick so she didn't go see him. She had tried calling him and even went to his apartment once but he wasn't there. She really had no idea where he was.

Jake pointed to an elaborate piece of science equipment taking up one whole corner of the lab, "This system automatically analyzes various aspects of tissue development. I need you to examine the computer files from October 23rd through yesterday for any abnormalities in the cultured tissue samples I took from Barney," commanded Jake.

Jennifer tilted her head sideways like a puppy and asked, "What am I looking for in particular?"

"Well anything out of the ordinary. I'll need you to compare previous samples with whatever sample you are currently looking at."

"Are you looking for your bacteria?"

"Not specifically, but if you see it in the auto-photographed specimens let me know. The system also automatically records any cellular changes whether they're enzymatic, chemical, or whatever. So just look for anything that stands out."

"Can't you get Blaine to look these over? I really need to study for an exam," pleaded Jennifer.

"I wouldn't trust Blaine with a dust mop, not after what he did for Lang..." Jake stopped before he said it.

"You mean my Dad right?" asked Jennifer, looking ashamed.

"Look Jennifer, I shouldn't be saying this but you and I both know that Blaine isn't the sharpest tool in the shed and I need someone who really knows what they're doing. I'd ask Ruben but..."

"Okay, okay, I get your meaning but I'm not staying past nine. If I don't finish reviewing your data I'll do it tomorrow," Jennifer conceded.

"Good, I have to get back to my office and finish preparing a lecture tomorrow morning. And Jennifer, don't stay too late."

"Don't worry professor, since Ruben's sick I don't have any reason to stay late," Jennifer said with a smile.

"What? Didn't you say he was in Texas?" Northrop asked while squinting his eyes and frowning.

"Yeah, he is." Jennifer said defensively.

"You just said he was sick."

"I meant his grandmother."

"Jennifer I need to know if anything's wrong with Ruben. Has he been sick?"

"No," said Jennifer, defiantly.

Jake reassured Jennifer, "He's not in any trouble. This is just between you and me. This is very important."

Jennifer struggled momentarily with her loyalties to Ruben and her concern over his well being. "He had the flu a little while back."

"How long ago Jennifer?"

"A week maybe two, I don't really remember I've been busy with school so I didn't think too much about it."

Jake stared uneasily at Jennifer and then down at the floor. "We should all be tested for exposure," Jake finally said.

Jennifer stood up. "Tested for what, the flu?"

Jake looked away for a moment before saying, "We need to be tested for the bacteria we've been working with."

Jennifer was clearly confused about the implications of Jake's statement.

"So what? It's harmless to us," Jennifer added.

"I recently uncovered evidence that may suggest the bacteria have…mutated and could be infectious," Jake explained rather uncomfortably.

"What? You knew this and didn't tell me! What about Ruben! He was bitten! Is that why you kept calling my phone that night? Is it?" yelled Jennifer.

"That's why I want you to review the data. Those samples are from an animal without immunosuppressant therapy. I want you to check them to see if the infection has spread to other areas."

"Spread to *other* areas? You mean that stupid freakin' rabbit had some crap that could hurt me! Oh my God!"

"No, that's not what I'm saying. I just need to see if we've had an immune response. We need blood samples from everyone exposed to the rabbits, Ruben included. Do you know where he is?"

"What, are you kidding me? I'm not going near that crap!" And no, he hasn't been answering his phone," Jennifer fumed as she folded her arms and turned her back to Jake.

Jake scratched his chin before saying, "Look, we've all been working with this bacteria for a long time. No one's sick. This is just a precaution. I want to see if we have antibodies to the bacteria. If we do, all it'll mean is that our bodies acknowledged it and then moved on. If we don't, then it's as I expected, the bacteria can't reproduce within us."

"But you said…"

"I'm a scientist Jennifer. This will put to rest any notion that our research is dangerous."

Jennifer nodded and ran her hands through her hair.

"Okay, first just let me get a sample of your blood and mine. We can look them over and then we can get Blaine down here to test him."

Jake fought hard to maintain the stiff posture of a scientist.

*I'm around my student. I have to maintain control. I have to be calm,* Jake didn't believe a word of what he'd just said.

After drawing their blood, Jake placed the slides containing the samples beneath the microscope and peered intently at them. He sat back in his chair and pressed his fingers together as he rested his forehead against them.

"Nothing, no sign of an elevated white blood-cell count." Jake said, sounding very relieved.

*Still, I'll have to do a full work-up before I can be sure. God this'll be a mind-numbing process, Jake thought.*

Jake turned on the T.V. and began the tedious process of conducting the blood panels.

"What are you doing? That's kind of bizarre don't you think?"

"Having a T.V. on in the background always helps me think. Just do what I told you and I'll do my job."

"Whatever," Jennifer shook her head and focused on the computer screen.

Jake Northrop was staring at the television with his mouth hanging open.

"Hysteria is sweeping Center City today as numerous accounts of random violence and looting are being reported. We go live now to the streets of downtown Philly to KNE reporter Dawn Phillips. Dawn, what can you tell our viewers about the reports we've been getting?"

"Charles all I can tell our viewers is that earlier this morning police began cordoning off sections of 9th and Market Street, including Terminal Market, about two blocks East of City Hall. We have been seeing E.M.T and other emergency personnel coming and going through the police barricades all day. In what may be an ominous sign, police have been steadily moving barricades in an ever-widening rectangle over the past hour. The quarantined area now covers nearly six whole city blocks and includes sections from Chestnut to Race and 7$^{th}$ to 13$^{th}$ Street. Police aren't commenting on the situation but we've spoken with people on the streets about the fear of an epidemic that seems to be somewhat contained right now to the affected areas mentioned. We recorded this interview earlier with Mike Berger who was working as a chef at the Reading Terminal Market."

"Mr. Berger what can you tell us about the situation in the market? What is happening in there?"

"Yeah, um, this dude was standing there in line and this lady just came up to him. I thought she was gonna kiss him or something. You know it was like she knew him. Anyway, he started screaming and that's when I saw his face. She tore off part of his face! She had blood all over her and she just stood there like nothing was wrong! I could see other people running around all over the market. Some people had blood on them and maybe chasing people or…I don't know, being chased. It was like they were all crazy or something," explained Mr. Berger.

"The same stories were told over and over again by those we interviewed. There seems to be some sort of hysteria or disease in the Market. This may be the worst outbreak of social violence Philadelphia has seen in recent history. We don't know if there's a biological or a chemical agent at work *or* if terrorism is involved. This has everybody down here on the streets very worried. Right now officials are warning curious onlookers to just stay away…wait a minute…*what was that? That sounded like…Charles, I don't know if our viewers can see this! Look at this! Pan your camera over there! Over there! Zoom in! Police seem to be firing at… a group of people! They appear to be clashing with the police! Can you see what we're seeing down here?"*

"It's difficult to make out but we see what appears to be a rioting mob. Can you tell us exactly where this is occurring?"

"It's outside the Market now! Whatever is happening has expanded beyond the barricades! Whoa! Oh my God! That was a huge explosion! Did you get that!? Tell me you got that! Can you see this!? Look at that fireball! Is that the police? Who is that?

They're coming! They're headed this way! We need to move! We need to move now! They're coming this way! We need to..."

"Dawn, can you hear me? Dawn? Are you still with us? It looks like we've lost the feed. For the viewers who've just tuned-in, we're following a situation unfolding in the area surrounding Terminal Market. Rioting began this evening as..."

Jake was no longer listening to the broadcast, *This can't be what I think it is. There's no way my bacteria is responsible for this. It couldn't be. How could all those people be infected with my bacteria?* Jake's stomach churned at the thought. He turned the T.V. off and noticed Jennifer was standing beside him.

"Oh my God what's happening professor?" Jennifer asked rather nervously.

"I'm not sure but I know someone who might. Stay put and continue looking at those sequences. Oh, and have Blaine come down so we can draw some blood."

"I don't want to stay here by myself professor. I'm really scared," moaned Jennifer.

"Look, just stay put. It's going to be dark soon. You're safe here in the lab. Besides, all the trouble is over in Center City," the professor said over his shoulder while walking out of the lab.

Jake had to make no less than four detours on what should've been a short drive over to the hospital. The police barricades and backed-up traffic had him driving in circles for an hour. When he was within sight of the hospital he parked his car and jogged through the haze of oppressive heat and stinging insects the rest of the way to the hospital entrance. There were people everywhere.

*Good God this place is packed! I hope they're not all... where is Heather?* he thought.

He quickly located the information desk and the answer to one of his questions. Heather was in the E.R. He walked down the hall toward the elevators but stopped when he saw a line of people waiting to board. Instead, he walked down the stairs to the ground floor. When he opened the door, an overwhelming volume of people waiting to be seen greeted him.

"What the hell is going on?" Jake said aloud.

He scanned the crowd for Heather but couldn't find her. He waded through throngs of coughing and wheezing people until he heard a familiar voice.

"Heather!" Jake shouted over the din of noise.

Heather looked around for the face to match the voice she had heard. A voice she hadn't heard for a long time but now more than ever, she longed to hear again.

"Jake, what are you doing here?"

"Looking for you. What's going on? I saw on the News that there's rioting down at Terminal. These people look sick, not injured. What is it? What's wrong with them?"

Heather looked around the crowd of people, raising her hands and shaking her head.

"We don't know. We've seen people coming in here sporadically for a few weeks with high fevers and flu-like symptoms. Then we started seeing people, young people in full cardiac arrest. It might be some sort of virus, I don't know. We also started seeing a lot of bite wounds and blunt-force trauma."

"Did you say bite wounds? What kind of animal made the wounds?"

"Mostly the human kind, serious wounds in many cases," Heather said as she nervously eyed the patients.

"Look Jake I'm sorry but I've gotta go. It's crazy around here."

"Hey, you think the bite wounds and this fever might have something to do with one another?"

Heather was walking toward the swinging E.R. doors but stopped.

"Yeah maybe, I saw a lady today in this very room bite one of the other patients. It took three security guards to restrain her. She was out of her mind. The patient she bit nearly bled to death. If he hadn't been in the E.R. waiting room when it happened he would've died. It was the scariest thing I've ever seen."

"What's that got to do with the fevers?"

"Jake I've gotta go."

Jake grabbed her arm and spun her toward him.

"Damn it this is important! I need to know what's wrong with them."

Heather frowned at him and yanked her arm away before saying, "Because I saw the same lady a week ago with the flu and a high fever. And…we've been short-handed because a lot of our staff has been calling in sick. Even Thompson, our Chief of Staff was out today."

"Can we go somewhere else to talk?"

"No! Jake can't you see I'm working, God what's wrong with you?"

"How are you…I mean have you been sick?"

"What? Jake… no I'm fine just a little tired."

Jake wrinkled his brow and said, "Heather I know when you're lying. I lived with you for eight years."

"Look I'm Fine. I had the flu a couple of weeks ago but I'm fine. Now I've gotta go."

Suddenly there was shouting. "Somebody help him! He's bleeding!" Carl Wurling had just stumbled into the waiting room.

Carl had made it to the hospital but just barely. He passed out as he entered the E.R. There were bite wounds all over Carl's left side and he was missing most of his left hand. Heather raced to him and tried to stop the bleeding.

"Carl! Carl! Wake up damn it! Don't you leave me! Don't leave me!" shouted Heather.

Jake wasn't sure what to do so he tried to comfort her but he failed miserably. He just felt cold and numb inside. He now believed that all of this was the result of his mutant bacteria. He didn't know how it had happened, he just knew it had.

*Pop! Pop! Pop!* Gunshots rang out and instantly there was screaming and general mayhem in the waiting area. Startled, Jake jerked his head over toward the noise. There were people; at least he thought they were people, attacking patients in the waiting area. Security guards were firing at the attackers but they continued their onslaught seemingly unaware that they were being shot! The smell of hospital disinfectant mingled with the smells of sweat, gunpowder, and…something else, putricene, and cadaverine. This was the smell of the dead.

“Heather we have to go now!” Jake commanded.

“I’m not leaving him here Jake!” screamed Heather.

“We’re not leaving him. He’s coming with us.”

Together they dragged Carl through the doors into the main hall of the hospital. Jake searched the halls frantically for a room that had something other than swinging doors.

“There!” Jake shouted. “Let’s get into that room and lock the doors behind us.”

There was a single patient in the room with them, an old lady who was quite alert for her age.

“What’s going on out there? I heard gunshots,” she asked in a quivering voice.

“Some crazy people have come into the hospital and they are being dealt with. Can you stand Miss?” Heather asked.

“Yes.”

“Good, we need to get this man onto the table. I have to stop his bleeding.”

“I’ll go sit in a chair,” the old lady offered as she stood.

Jake and Heather hefted Carl onto the table and Heather began first aid. There were enough supplies in the room that Heather was able to stitch-up most of Carl’s wounds. His hand, or what was left of it, was a different story. It would have to be amputated but she couldn’t do that here. At least she stopped the hemorrhaging. He was stable for now and that would have to do.

Shots were infrequent now and they sounded much farther away. Within the hospital, they could still hear screams, horrible screams and people pleading and begging for their lives.

“Jake do you have a phone? We need to call 911.”

Jake dialed the number but got a busy signal. He then quickly dialed home and heard his own voice on the answering machine.

“Hello, I’m unavailable at the moment but if you could leave…” Jake hung up before his message could finish.

“I can’t get through Heather. I keep getting a busy signal. The lines are open though. I was able to call my house.”

Jake then called the University so he could warn Jennifer.

“Hello,” replied a gravelly voice from the other end of the phone.

"Blaine is that you?"

"No."

"Ruben, thank God you're okay! Look I need to warn you about…"

"We already know," Ruben interrupted.

"We? Who else is there with you? Ruben, hello? Damn it the line went dead." A loud scream in the distance reminded Jake of their current situation.

"We need to get out of here!" Jake exclaimed in a loud whisper. "Miss, can you walk?" Jake directed his question towards the old lady without looking away from Heather. There was only silence and the far away drone of screams and shouts.

"Miss?" Jake repeated as he turned toward the old lady.

She sat in the chair, her eyes unblinking and glazed over in death.

"Heather, she's dead."

"What? Oh no, she must have had a heart attack."

Jake turned slowly toward Heather and said, "I'm not so sure."

He squinted and walked toward the dead women.

"Heather, she has a bite wound on her…"

Jake's report was cut short by a loud slamming noise against the door. Jake jumped and then held his finger up to his lips.

Heather understood. The banging continued and then came a weak cry for help. "Jake someone's out there." Heather said in a hushed tone.

Jake moved toward the door and asked, "Are you okay? Are you alone?"

The voice replied, "Yes, but those things are out here and I'm hurt. Please let me in," the voice cried.

"Jake we've got to let her in."

As Heather reached for the door, Carl's voice cried, "Look out Heather!"

"Shit!" screamed Jake.

The old lady was up and moving towards Jake. She wore a blank expression until her mouth slowly twisted into an awful grimace showing her brown teeth. Jake grabbed a chair and swung it in front of the old lady. She didn't slow her advance. A loud crack rang out as the next swing connected square with the old lady. Gurgling noises and sounds of raw meat falling on the ground echoed in the otherwise dead-silent room, as the old lady fell.

Carl Wurling was attempting to sit up and warn Jake and Heather, “She’s not alive. She’s not going to stop!”

Carl had pieced enough of the puzzle together to realize they weren’t dealing with psychotic individuals.

“You’ve gotta get out of here! Don’t let them bite you or scratch you! They’re infected with something! Heather, I love you. I’m so sorry.”

“I won’t leave you here Carl!” Heather cried out.

“Go! Get away from here!” Carl screamed weakly.

The old lady was standing again. Her head was at an unnatural angle to the rest of her body and congealing blood was beginning to spill from her nose, mouth and the tear in her neck. Jake brought the chair down on the old lady again and again. It did not stop her. Jake grabbed Heather and attempted to open the door with the other hand.

“No!” Heather screamed as she grasped Jake’s arm.

Jake pointed to the zombie and said, “Do you see that? I can’t stop it and there’s a lot more where that came from out there,” he said, now pointing towards the E.R. waiting area.

“We *cannot* carry Carl through this! We can’t! *He* knows it! That’s why he told you to leave. We tried. We did what we could and now he wants us to go. Heather *I* need you damn it! Let’s go!”

Heather’s tortured words echoed into the hallway, “I love you Carl! I’m sorry. Forgive me!”

“I forgive you! Now let’s go! They’re right behind me damn it!” said Mary, the voice behind the door.

Mary was new at the hospital but Heather recognized her.

“You wouldn’t let me in and I almost ran away but I heard you arguing about leaving so I stayed.”

“We’re both thrilled that you decided to stay but right now we have to go,” Jake said sarcastically.

The frightened crew began running down the hall through the hospital toward the Gibbon Building on Sansom and 11th street. This was their only way out.

Staff and security were nowhere to be found and only a few patients wandered the halls or called out for help from their rooms. None of these people were critical care patients and they were quite capable of leaving the building. Unfortunately, they had no idea the danger they were in or they were just too frightened to do anything about it. Jake told them they needed to leave and asked that they come along. There were few takers.

Just as well. I can't protect everybody and all of these people would only slow us down, Jake thought.

"Let's move along people; we have to go! There's a whole lotta trouble behind us and you don't want to get caught up in it. Let's go! Keep moving!"

Jake had no time to explain. The people that chose to stay behind simply couldn't believe something so insidious had been unleashed upon their world. He also knew that they would most likely perish and join the horde of zombies that now plagued Center City. If he had time to think about it, he would've been paralyzed by guilt. Nobody in the group had any idea what was really happening. But Jake knew. What was worse, he knew there was no treatment for those infected with *Zombacter*, no cure, and no vaccine.

Once someone is bitten, it's only a matter of time. But how had so many become infected so quickly? No time for that kind of thinking now. I must stay focused. We have to get out of here, Jake's mind wandered.

"What are those things? Are they people?" asked Mary while they were jogging toward the elevator.

"Yeah they're people alright," Jake replied.

"What the hell's wrong with them?" Mary continued her barrage of questions. "Why are they doing this?"

Jake interrupted her, "Mary, you're going to have to trust me on this. These people are infected with a fatal disease and they are compelled to spread it to others. That's why they are biting healthy people they come into contact with."

"How do you know all this? How do we stop them? Some of those people back there looked, well...like they...well they were green! Are the police coming to help us? Hasn't any body called them?" Mary said while gasping for breath.

"We can talk about this later. Right now we have to go," barked Jake.

He knew the police wouldn't be coming. He'd tried to call many times but kept getting a busy signal. The internet was still working but it was no help at the moment. He reached the elevator first and quickly punched the up arrow. Long seconds went by as the group stood silently waiting for the elevator.

"What's taking the elevator so long," asked a patient who chose to come along.

"We need to take the stairs," Heather said forcefully. "What's your name?" she directed her question toward the patient who asked about the elevator.

"Sue Goldstein," she said.

"Sue, I'm Heather. I'm a nurse here," Heather said, introducing herself. "This is Jake and that's Mary."

"Hello," Sue replied. "This is Gary but we call him Jameson. He works with computers and that fellow behind Mary is Shams. Well, his real name is too hard to say so we all call him Shams."

"Shhh, be quiet for a second. I hear something," Jake commanded.

There was a dull thudding noise coming from the stairwell above their heads.

"What is it?" asked Shams.

"Shut up!" Jake hissed.

The rhythmic sound continued as they tried to figure out its source.

"Hey, take my gun. It's only a .22 but it'll stop someone causing trouble," Shams said.

Gratefully, Jake reached out his hand and convincingly hid his surprise over the sudden appearance of a gun.

"Thanks," he said with a lopsided grin.

Alone, Jake walked up the stairs and out of site of the hospital survivors. The landing was just above his head now and the noise was much louder than before. He continued walking toward the landing and shook his head from side to side while grimacing.

There he stood on the landing with the blood pounding in his ears and no one to save his ass. It was just him and whatever lay beyond that door.

Jake gritted his teeth and hissed, "Shit!"

He stood there contemplating his options for what seemed like an eternity. There *was* no other option.

"Here we go!"

*Boom!* The door slammed open as Jake's foot followed through on a well-placed kick. Jake swung the gun out in front of him and moved it frantically from side to side. His breathing was so heavy now that he couldn't hear anything else. Some of the flickering fluorescent light fixtures hanging down from the ceiling were creating a surreal stroboscopic effect. Jake quickly surveyed the second floor and tried to focus on movements directly to his left. It nearly came too late as several hulking forms rushed him from the shadows. Instinctively, Jake pointed and pulled the trigger. *Pop! Pop! Pop!* The figures became people and they grew larger and reached out toward Jake. Cold sweat appeared instantly all over his body. Something inside told him to fire at their heads. Maybe it was his research or maybe it was their twisted faces and empty rotting stares but all the same he fired. *Pop! Pop! Pop!*

*Was that all of them? Did I get 'em? I can't hear anything. Am I alive? Shit!* The thoughts tumbled over one another in his head.

Aside from the infected rabbits, he had never killed anything larger than a cockroach. There lay two corpses not fifteen feet away. One looked like he was old enough to be his grandfather and the other couldn't have been more than twelve. A great sadness welled up within Jake Northrop. It was sadness rife with the bitter taste of guilt and regret. All these were things he couldn't change and couldn't take back. How could he ever explain this to the boy's mother? He thought for only a moment and concluded that she probably wasn't alive either.

*These things were already dead. All I can try to do is save whoever is not infected,* He reasoned.

Jake didn't have much time alone with his thoughts before he was knocked over sideways. His mind reeled from the shock. His attention focused on a rather large set of teeth that were intent on taking his nose.

*Where's my gun?* He thought as he struggled to hold back the darkness that threatened to consume him.

It was too strong. Only seconds had passed but his muscles had begun to burn long ago and were now slowly giving up.

*Son of a bitch they're strong!* A part of Jake's mind marveled at the strength and intensity with which these things mercilessly pursued their prey. He was beginning to think that he deserved this fate. He was giving up. He couldn't hold it back any longer, then abruptly the weight of his assailant was mercifully gone.

*What happened?* Jake thought.

He realized the entire rescued crew had been watching him. He glanced over at the lifeless form that now lie in a heap beside him and saw a metal pole neatly penetrating either side of its skull.

"We've gotta keep moving Jake!" a familiar voice shouted.

*Heather?*

He had barely made it to his feet when gurgling screams erupted all around him.

*This can't be happening!* Jake's mind screamed.

He grabbed the closest thing he could find and began swinging it wildly in front of him as he advanced through the ranks of the infected and undead. Again, shots rang out in the hospital. *Clack-clack-clack-clack-clack!* Instinctively Jake fell to the floor and covered his head. That was no handgun; it was the sound of an assault rifle! Looking up he saw a half-dozen zombies fall in front of him.

*The National Guard is here!* Jake shouted in his mind. His outlook on the whole situation immediately brightened.

He began speaking loudly and clearly even before he stood, "I'm Doctor Northrop. I'm a scientist from the University!"

"Well Doc, you can call me Bill. I see you got yourself one hell of a zombie problem," Bill said with a sardonic grin.

"Who are you? Where's the Guard?" Jake replied in rapid succession.

Bill's grin disappeared so quickly that Jake wasn't sure if he ever really saw it.

"I don't think there comin'."

Jake's heart sank at hearing this bit of news.

"I think the riot police and S.W.A.T. teams, or whoever they were, left. The ones that got trapped down here are probably dead by now."

Bill was scanning the room like a soldier and that's when Jake noticed Bill had only one arm. He looked somewhat familiar in his blue denim jacket but Jake couldn't place his face. The man looked rough, worn, weather-beaten, and used up.

"Don't I know you?" asked Jake.

Before Bill could answer, Jameson butted in and said smugly, "He's a bum! I've seen him bumming change over near Market."

Frowning, Jake shot Jameson an unforgiving stare and began walking toward him.

"That man just saved all of our lives and you're so ignorant that you insulted him for his troubles?"

Jake backhanded Jameson not once but twice: the second time for looking indignant after the first slap.

"Apologize to Bill, now you asshole!" Jake fumed.

"I…I'm sorry. I didn't mean to…"

Bill stopped Jameson before he could finish.

"It's all good. I know you didn't mean nothin' by it."

All the attention actually made him feel embarrassed.

"We're all grateful to you Bill. Can you tell us if there's someplace safe we can go for the night?" asked Heather while shooting Jake looks of disapproval and interest at the same time.

"Ah, yes ma'am. I think we can hide safely down in the tunnels."

"I need to go back to the University. Usually, there aren't many people hanging around there this time of evening. And I told a student of mine to stay put until I got back," Jake said, redirecting Bill's plan.

"How does it look out there? Do you think we can get to the University?" asked Heather.

"Yeah, it's not far and I'd rather take my chances out there than stay in here."

"Why the hell should we go to the University? Why don't we just get out of the city?" Sue asked.

"Well for one thing the part of the city we're in is under quarantine and in case you haven't noticed, there's a shitload of dead people running around out there."

"You have a gun! You can protect us. Let's get outta here!" Jameson blurted.

"I'd like to leave this city as much as you but an M16 only carries thirty rounds. I imagine between me and that poor fellow that had it before me… hell there're only about twelve left. I don't think that little pea-shooter *he's* holdin is gonna do much good either," Bill said gesturing toward Shams who had just found his gun lying beside a corpse.

"Nah, it's empty. I don't have another clip," Shams sighed with regret.

"Do you have any idea how hard it is to hit their heads with one shot? It's the only way to put 'em down for good, took me a few wasted rounds to figure that one out. It's at least two miles to get across the Delaware. How many of those things do you think we'd run into before we crossed the bridge?" Bill asked.

"O…kay, but wouldn't we have to go across the Schuykill Bridge to get out of Center City…to…get to the University?" Jameson reasoned.

Bill stared coldly at Jameson without speaking.

"Look, we gotta get out of Center City whichever way we go right? We don't have to head for Jersey. Why don't we just go…" Jameson continued before Jake interrupted him.

"Enough! You can go where you like but I'm going to the University. Anybody that wants to come along better hurry because I'm leaving *now*!" Jake barked.

"I'm goin' with you Doc." Bill answered. "How far is it to the University?"

"It's a fairly straight shot about two miles East of here," answered Jake.

"You're out of your minds! That's just as far away as Jersey!" Jameson complained.

"Yes it is but I have equipment at the lab that might just save our collective asses."

"Is there something you're not telling us about those things?" Shams chimed in.

Everyone was holding their breath and looking at Jake. He looked at each of their faces in turn while considering how to break the news to them.

"Yeah, I know a lot about those things. I know what they are and why they're attacking people. They're infected with a kind of bacteria. It was designed to create a bio-computer. The bacteria align themselves with neural networks of a host and then take over. The stuff kills its host but the bacteria don't die. They continue controlling the host's body. The only reason those things bite people is to spread the bacteria-continuation of the species you see. The only thing I don't understand is how they all got infected."

"How the hell do you know all of this?" Bill asked.

"Because I'm the one that created this mess," Jake retorted staring directly at Bill.

"Something went wrong and I was trying to figure it all out when my boss went behind my back and attempted to destroy my research. The bacteria I created was mishandled and escaped into the community."

Bill dropped down into a chair and stared blankly at the floor.

"Look, I know you have no reason to trust me, especially after what I've just told you, but I have someone back at the University studying this stuff. I think I can develop a vaccine of sorts, or at least a combination of antibiotics that can help. Bill is that a grenade launcher on that rifle?"

Bill looked up, still in shock over what he had just heard.

He shook his head and said, "Don't look like a grenade launcher to me. It don't work anyway. I think it might be just for looks or somethin'. I tried it earlier but it only made a humming noise and nothin' happened."

"Is that a battery pack on the stock?" Jake inquired.

"I dunno Doc. You got me."

"May I borrow that for a moment?" Jake asked with his arms outstretched.

"Sure."

"You idiot! You're gonna let the man who created all of those zombies have your gun! You imbecile!" Jameson shouted.

"He didn't make the damn zombies you little shit! He's the only one here who knows anything about 'em. So I suggest you listen to 'im," Bill admonished Jameson, his eyes glinting in the light like two pieces of obsidian.

Jake looked the weapon over for several minutes and had to ask Bill what functions the various components served.

Finally Jake announced, "I have some good news. This is not a grenade launcher it's an E.M.P. weapon."

"Well whoop tee doo," Jameson said while twirling his upraised pointer finger in circles.

Agitated, Jake explained the importance of the weapon, "This is an electromagnetic pulse rifle."

Jake's pronouncement was met with blank stares.

"Look, with a regular gun it takes a direct shot to the head to stop one of these…zombies."

Jake hated using the word zombie. He felt like the word should only be mentioned in the context of a crappy horror movie.

He continued, "But with this, you can stop dozens with a single shot even if you have bad aim. It won't…kill them, but it should buy you enough time to say, run down the street and to safety."

"How's it work Doc?" asked Bill

"It interferes with the way the bacteria communicate, or at least I hope it will." "You hope it will work? You don't even know do you?" Jameson sneered.

Ignoring Jameson Jake added, "Once I get back to my lab I think I can make more of these based on this design. Shall we go then?"

"Well then I guess we're all going." Sue conceded rather acidly.

"Unless you want to stay here," Jake directed at Sue.

"Bill, you'd better take the lead. Oh and here's your rifle." Jake advised as he handed the weapon over to Bill.

The group moved slowly out onto 11th Street through the shattered remains of the hospital entrance and headed north toward Chestnut, staying well clear of the E.R. The air was dank, heavy and still thick with biting insects. The only breeze to speak of came when a car loaded with people crashed past them, zigzagging through the maze of abandoned vehicles.

*Probably looters, best not draw their attention,* Jake thought.

He knew they couldn't go back to the parking garage where his own car was parked. It wouldn't make any difference; most of the streets were now clogged with abandoned cars. If they all piled into one of *them,* it could become a deathtrap. No, it was much faster on foot. It was likely that they might run into more survivors they could join up with. It was a big city and surely those buildings were filled with scared but otherwise healthy people.

They kept close to the buildings as they inched along; moving out toward the center of Walnut Street whenever they came near a storefront. Fires burned sporadically around the city and gunshots and screams could be heard in the distance. It was going to be a long night.

"At least the electricity is still on," Bill said to Jake.

"How did you end up down at the hospital tonight Bill?" Jake asked while they were waiting for the rest of the group to cross an intersection.

"I should ask you the same question." Bill looked at Jake for a few seconds and then with his back against the wall, looked over his shoulder scanning the sidewalks and buildings ahead of them.

Without turning again toward Jake, he began speaking in a subdued manner. "I was making sure someone got the help they needed."

"Who?"

"Some guy that got attacked by a…one of those things. Said he was a doctor. His name was Carl I believe."

"Carl Wurling?"

"Yeah, you know 'im?"

"You could say that. What happened?"

"I don't know. It don't seem real. A few weeks ago, a buddy of mine ate somethin' that made 'im sick. Got it out of a dumpster over by Terminal. I told 'im not to eat it but he was hungry and..."

"What was it?"

"What do you mean what was it?" Bill was clearly irritated by the interruption.

"What did he get out of the dumpster?"

"It was a rabbit, well most of a rabbit. Damn thing was frozen solid. He didn't cook it right."

Jake's heart nearly stopped. He was suddenly aware that Bill was staring at him.

"What's wrong Doc? Look like you've seen a ghost."

"Hey, come on. Let's get moving. We keep hearing noises behind us." Mary urged.

Bill continued his story as they walked, speaking in hushed tones. Jake made sure he was close enough to catch all of the details. He couldn't believe what he was hearing.

"I kept tellin' Marvin to go to the hospital but he wouldn't listen, never did. I thought he had food poisonin' or somethin'...maybe a stomach flu. He disappeared for a while. I kept going over to the market to check on 'im but he what'n nowhere to be found. Early this evenin' I went back to see if I could find 'im and I did. He'd changed. He looked... well now I know but then...he just looked real bad, smelled real bad. He tried to attack me and so I started to run. That's when I saw 'im get Carl. Poor bastard was in the wrong place you know."

Bill paused for a minute before saying, "Marvin's dead. He was dead before I shot 'im. Thinkin' back I should've known somthin' wasn't right. What the hell was S.W.A.T. doin' downtown anyhow." Bill shook his head while looking at the ground.

"Tough old bird... let me tell ya brother, he killed two of those S.W.A.T. boys before I took 'im down. That's how I ended up with this."

Jake could barely make out Bill's toothless grin as he turned and held up the M16. His grin faded quickly and his eyes grew large as he hissed under his breath.

"Get down!" Bill yelled, motioning at the same time. He took aim at something directly behind Sue.

"Don't shoot! Don't shoot! It's me, Carl."

"Carl!" Heather shouted.

Jameson grabbed her arm, effectively preventing her from running to him. "He doesn't look so good."

"How the hell did you make it out of the hospital?" asked Jake.

"I rubbed some of their… putrefied remains on me to mask my scent and it worked. I don't know where I got the idea. It's weird… they pretty much ignored me… Those things would run up to me and…smell me or something I don't know…and then just turn away uninterested. I don't think they eat carrion," Carl said, gasping for breath. "I took some morphine…I'm not feeling too much pain right now…but I'm very weak. I kept trying to catch up with you guys… but I didn't want to yell and draw attention."

"Christ you stink Carl," Jake said while pinching his nose shut.

Jake and Heather looked at each other simultaneously, a silent agreement passing between them. Carl noticed it too.

"I know I'm infected Jake…but I may be of some assistance until…well, it takes about two weeks I'm guessing from the patients we've seen in the E.R. You're not in any danger from me for the time being."

It was the first time Carl had addressed Northrop directly. Jake was taken aback by Carl's openness.

"Look Carl, you can come with us to the University. Maybe I can help you."

"Are you out of your *mind*?" Jameson raged through clinched teeth.

"*He* is *not* coming with us! He'll get us all killed! *He's* infected! What if *he* bleeds on me?" he continued, thrusting his finger toward Carl.

"Hold it right there! Drop that gun!" Damn looters! Drop it now!" A voice shouted from the entrance to a liquor store that was about fifteen yards in front of Bill.

The man was aiming a very large pistol directly at them while looking around nervously.

"Mr. we're not looters. We're just tryin' to get to the University. This fellow behind me is a professor over there," Bill calmly explained.

While the man was arguing with Bill, Jake noticed someone on the sidewalk approaching the shopkeeper from behind.

"Hey look out behind you! There's someone behind you!" the professor yelled.

"What, do you think I'm stupid? Just shut up! I swear I'll blow your head off if you keep talking!" the shop-keeper ranted.

Bill hadn't lowered his weapon and neither had the other man.

"Mr. we don't want any trouble, we'll just be on our way okay?"

Now the approaching shadow was close enough to the illuminated storefront for everyone to see it clearly. It was no man, not anymore. A putrid greenish-black color, this thing had long since been dead and was missing portions of its face and neck. They tried to warn the shopkeeper before it attacked but to no avail. The zombie tore into the man's shoulder. Screaming in pain, he fired his gun straight into Jake's group. He fired twice more before Bill dropped the man and the zombie with two well-placed shots.

Jake and Bill looked back at the group of people they were protecting. Heather and Jameson were down. Carl was already at Heather's side.

Jake nearly leapt over Sue to get to Heather.

"Heather! Oh no! No-no, no, no, no! Come on baby, hang on you're gonna be alright. Carl, help her!" pleaded Jake.

"I can't! I don't want to infect her. Put your hand over the wound. No, you have to press down hard Jake!" Carl instructed.

"I am damn it! It won't stop! It won't stop! What do I do Carl? Help me!" Jake was frantic.

A geyser of blood spurted out from around Jakes' hand as he tried to reposition himself to stop the bleeding. The bullet had ripped through the left side of Heather's chest. She was dying right in front of the two men that loved her. Heather's eyes were wide with terror. She coughed, splashing blood all over Jake's face. She was trying to swallow the blood back down. Heather was drowning almost as fast as she was bleeding to death. With a pleading look, her eyes darted over to Carl and then fell back on Jake. She tried to speak but only managed a horrible gurgling noise as blood poured from her mouth. Carl pressed the back of his hand into his mouth and began whimpering pitifully. He knew she was not going to make it.

"What do I do? Carl help us! What do I do? No, don't go baby. Hang on. No, I love you. I've always loved you. Don't leave me Heather! *Nooo*! God, No! Don't do this to me! Don't *you do this to me*! Oh God Heather, nooo!" Jake's pleas broke down into pitiful sobs.

Heather closed her eyes and then she was gone.

# PSYCHOSIS

**November 28**
**Desert outside Williams, Arizona:**

Sheriff Roy Clay was very upset and confused. He couldn't remember how he'd ended up in the middle of the Arizona desert with blood on his clothes. It was dark and he was standing near his patrol car on a dusty, dirt road. His head was pounding and he felt like throwing-up. There was a horrible metallic taste in his mouth, like a mixture of blood and bile. Roy hadn't quite gotten over the flu he had battled a week ago and he still felt weak. In fact, the sheriff hadn't felt right since then. He struggled desperately to recall anything that might explain his current situation. Suddenly, his police radio crackled to life and Roy jumped.

"Sheriff, come in! We have a situation here at the station! Sheriff, come in!"

Roy opened the patrol car door and sat down in the driver's seat, messaging his temples.

"What's up Marge?" He said into the microphone.

His ears were ringing loudly and he found it difficult to concentrate. He listened for a few seconds to the hiss of static popping in the speakers and quickly grew tired of it.

"Marge, go ahead," the sheriff said impatiently.

Still there was nothing but static coming from the speakers.

"Just what I need," Roy said sullenly.

He then tried to raise his deputy on the radio with no luck. Roy slammed down the CB, started the car and began driving when he realized he had no idea which direction to travel. He continued driving until he saw a sign that read N. Highway 64. It wasn't a long stretch of highway between the sheriff and the police station in Williams, Arizona but it was long enough to annoy Roy Clay. He cursed the radio for not being able to reach anyone and his head hurt so badly he could barely stand it. He didn't have a mobile phone so he could only fume.

Roy searched his mind to try and understand what had happened. Abruptly a vision flashed before him. In his mind 's eye, he was walking toward the back of an old, rusty, powder-blue Dodge with a Navajo Nation license plate. But just as quickly as it had come, the image in his mind vanished leaving Roy with more questions than answers.

As he drove, more scenes were replayed in his mind. He heard a woman screaming and then he saw a man with long, black braids that trailed down his back lying facedown on the ground. A pool of blood was forming around his neck and a red stain began to creep up and around the collar of his white, button-down shirt. Roy snapped out of his vision but remained disoriented, just as if someone had prematurely awakened him from a dream.

*What the hell's happening to me? I gotta get some rest before I lose it.*

He stopped his patrol car at a convenience store just outside of town and stepped out to fill the gas tank. The image of the Navajo man was haunting him and he couldn't shake the feeling that something terrible had happened. Roy went to pay for the gas and realized his wallet was missing.

"Outstanding," he said in a voice dripping with sarcasm.

"Sheriff, are you alright? Are you hurt?" The store owner knew the sheriff and was very concerned about him

"Yeah…no, I don't really know. I blacked-out or something and I ended up out in the desert," Roy explained while rubbing the top of his head.

"We gotta get you to a doctor sheriff. You might have got whacked on the head by someone."

"I think you're right. I can't remember anything. I keep tryin' to radio the station but all I get's static. Could you give 'em a call for me….uh…"

"Charlotte, sheriff, I'm Charlotte. Don't you remember me?"

"I'm sorry Charlotte, of course I remember you," Roy said with a forced smile.

At this point he barely knew who he was let alone this store owner.

"I'll radio the station but I'm calling the hospital too 'cause you don't look so good. Why don't you just sit down back here by the fan and I'll bring you some ice-cold water, okay dear?"

"Alright Charlotte, you're the boss."

Suddenly the sheriff was thrust into the nightmarish world of another vision—

He was lying in his tent in the desert trying to ride out a severe thunderstorm. The wind was howling and threatening to blow his shelter away. The fiberglass tent poles began to fold under the onslaught of the storm. This caused the polyester taffeta to beat down inches from his face with a loud fluttering noise. Every now and then the wind would let up and the tent would recoil under the stress of the bent fiberglass poles and snap back into position. It would quickly fold down on top of him again as soon as the wind speed increased. Suddenly, the zipper of his tent gave way and the flap flew open.

Lightning flashed outside and briefly illuminated the desert beyond the billowing entrance to his tent. A woman appeared in the doorway. In the darkness, the sheriff could make out the smooth curves of a silhouette that could not be mistaken for anyone else. She knelt down in the entrance and stretched her body into the tent with him. Roy knew that body. It was his deputy, Joy Ferguson. His fantasy had come true. She silently crawled on top of Roy and he wrapped his arms around her.

He was going to kiss her when the lightening flared. It was terrifying. The lightening illuminated the most disgusting thing ever upchucked from the depths of hell. It was a putrid corpse with all manner of insect larvae creeping from the tiny rotting orifices that speckled its body. Its swollen eyes were pinkish-brown and it exuded pus from the many tears and holes in its decaying, greenish-gray flesh. Abruptly, it stuck what was left of its tongue into his mouth. Screaming, Roy bit down and threw the thing off him.

He searched frantically for his gun but couldn't find it. To his horror, Roy remembered that he'd left it in his car. The creature came at him again. Instinctively, Roy punched the thing in its face and it screamed hideously. This was his chance to escape. Roy ran to his car and retrieved his gun. He then braced his arm atop the open car door and stared into the torrential rain. He tried to get a fix on his tent or the thing that had been inside of it but couldn't see anything. With the next lightening flash he saw his quarry, the thing was moving toward him. With two loud pops, the creature fell—

When the sheriff awoke from his vision, he was standing on the sidewalk in front of the convenience store. His head was pounding worse than ever. His uniform was spattered with fresh blood and he had no idea how he ended up outside. Roy walked back into the store to look for the owner and began calling her name.

"Charlotte! Charlotte! Where are you? Look I think I know what..." The sheriff was so surprised to see the store owner huddled in the corner with blood on her face and arms that he forgot what he was going to say.

"Oh my God what happened to you?"

"Ahhgggg! Get away from me you freak! You sick bastard! Help! Somebody help me!" she screamed in a cigarette- and whiskey-ravaged voice.

"Charlotte it's me Roy. I'm not going to hurt you. Jesus Christ, who did this to you?"

Charlotte started sobbing uncontrollably and lowered her head, resigned to the fate that awaited her.

Without looking up, she said in a broken voice, "You need help sheriff. I'm so sorry but you do."

Roy didn't understand what she meant.

"Charlotte you have to tell me what happened."

She looked up at Roy and he could see that she had a nasty gash just below her left eye and blood was pouring down her neck.

"I'm just an old lady that don't mean you any harm. Please don't hurt me anymore. Please, please don't hurt me anymore," Charlotte begged in the most pitiful and humble manner a human being is capable of and then started sobbing again.

Roy began to recall his encounter with her and started to shake. He saw himself beating her and then... it became blurry again. Roy's chest tightened and as he clutched at it, he felt something wet in his shirt pocket. Shaking, he reached into it and found an object that was slick and rubbery. He pulled the thing out and stared dumbly at it. He couldn't tell what it was at first and then… he knew.

"Oh my God! Oh my God!"

He threw it on the ground while stepping backward until he ran into a wall. The sheriff was groaning and wiping his hands on the sides of his pants.

"No, no, no, no, no."

The visions kept coming. For Roy there would be no relief. He remembered killing the Navajo man and his daughter for no reason in particular. He tore the man's throat out with his bare hands and then sexually assaulted his daughter. The sheriff was crying and holding his hands over his face. He began to stagger out of the store when another truth nearly leveled him. It was a nightmare from which he could not awake and it would only get worse. The poor sheriff recalled what had really happened last night in the desert—

Joy Ferguson was kissing him passionately. They were in his tent and it was dark except for the dim light coming from his small clock radio. A classic song by Journey was playing. Roy was still in his uniform but he wouldn't be for long if Joy had anything to say about it. He had dreamed of this moment ever since the first time he saw her.

*She's so beautiful and an officer of the law to boot,* he thought.

He had been feeling so crummy that he almost decided not to ask Joy to go camping with him. He was glad he didn't. Except for his headache, Roy was having the time of his life. He never wanted this moment to end. If he died right here, right now he would have lived a full life. It was then he began to feel strange. A horrible suspicion crept into Roy's mind.

*Why is she suddenly interested in me?* Roy thought to himself.

This is what he had always wanted but she had never let on to being remotely interested in him. It was odd. After all, Roy was the one who talked her into camping out in the desert but now Joy was the one in command.

*Why had she insisted on following him in her own car?* Roy felt very uncomfortable and extremely paranoid. The hair on the back of his neck stood up and uncontrollable fear flooded his body. For some reason he knew that his deputy was trying to kill him. He had to act now or it would all be over. At that instant Roy bit down on Joy's tongue and then threw her off of him. In shock, she howled in pain. The sheriff searched for his gun but it wasn't there. He had to neutralize the threat. Roy punched Joy in the face as hard as he could and then bolted from the tent. He grabbed his gun from the car and waited for his deputy. Roy's head was pounding and the ringing in his ears had grown so loud that he couldn't see straight.

"There you are! I'm warning you! Don't come any closer!" Roy growled at his deputy stumbling out of the tent.

*Pop! Pop!* She collapsed on the ground.

The dense fog of the vision had lifted and Roy was again lucid and in the present. He staggered and swayed like a drunkard. He'd done the unthinkable. Roy fell to his knees and puked on the sidewalk. Understanding there was nothing left of the life he'd known; Roy unholstered his gun to stop the pain once and for all.

Marge was applying pressure to Joy's gunshot wound when her radio crackled.

"Help me! Is anybody there! Oh God, please help me!"

It was Charlotte; she had finally gotten through to someone. Marge couldn't risk taking her hand off the wound again. It was bad but if she could stop the bleeding, the deputy should survive.

"You're gonna be okay kid. I just gotta get this bleeding stopped."

Joy nodded her head in agreement. She didn't want to try and speak. Her tongue was deeply bitten and it was much more painful than the gunshot wound in her arm. She hung her head over the wastebasket and allowed the blood to drain from her mouth. It'd already ruined the lacy, lingerie tank top she was wearing but she couldn't stand it running down her chest. Joy was still in shock over what had happened and couldn't understand why Roy had attacked her. She had been in love with him, she still was. He was clearly ill but Joy hadn't yet connected the dots.

"I've called the hospital Joy and they're on their way. I keep trying to raise the sheriff but he's not answering."

At this last statement, Joy shot straight up, grabbed Marge by the arm and shook her head from side to side.

"Okay, okay, I won't call him again," Marge said looking very worried.

The radio came back to life as Charlotte again begged for help.

"I've gotta get this kiddo. Can you stand?" Marge asked Joy.

Joy nodded and they both walked over to the radio.

"Go ahead Charlotte."

"Help me! The sheriff's gone crazy, he attacked me and…and…he bit my ear off!" moaned Charlotte.

The rest of the story was lost between the sounds of her crying and the static of an old radio.

Joy had gone so pale that when Marge looked back at her she gasped. She looked back at the radio and composed herself.

"We'll send the paramedics right over Charlotte. You hang in their honey okay?

"Hurry, please!" Charlotte cried.

"Is…is the sheriff still there with you Charlotte?" Marge asked reluctantly.

"I don't know. He went outside. He acted like he didn't remember doing any of this to me. He's crazy! Just hurry, please!"

Everything clicked into place for Joy. She suddenly realized that the sheriff must've been infected with rabies or something after he was bitten by the man that night at the *No Tell Motel*. She snatched a pen off the desk and began scribbling a note for Marge that read:

*Call troopers…Tell them not to shoot him… Don't hurt him… Use Taser… He doesn't know what he's doing. Be careful… He's armed and dangerous! Don't let him bite or scratch you…Has rabies!*

While reading the note, a frown creased Marge's forehead and face. She looked up at Joy and said, "Oh my dear child. It was him wasn't it, that did this to you? Oh my goodness."

Joy's shoulders began to shake as she cried silently.

# THE VETERINARIAN

**November 28**
**Center City:**

Ever since Jill Sorenson was a small child, she had always wanted to visit Australia. Now she would get her chance. Jill had made all of the arrangements for her trip. She hated having to kennel Ramone but she couldn't bring her dog on the flight. The veterinarian's conference would begin in five days. This would give her plenty of time to enjoy the flight and the see the country. After what she had been through the last couple of weeks she was looking forward to a little getaway.

Jill guessed that the flu was making it difficult for her to sleep. Her extremities would spasm just as she was drifting off and she would awake with a start. Maybe her inability to sleep was caused by the horrible migraines she had been suffering or maybe it was because of the loud ringing in her ears, both of which began during her illness. But that awful sound in her head wasn't tinnitus. It was a garbled noise, a high-pitched whine like thousands of flies buzzing around a rotting carcass on a hot summer day. Jill, always the pragmatist, thought it was simply fluid build-up in her inner ears.

Eventually, sleep for Jill Sorenson came almost without warning. She was constantly groggy now, in a fog of sorts. If she closed her eyes for more than a few seconds a warm tingling sensation would flow through her body and she would awake several hours later in some other part of her house, completely disoriented.

When she first started experiencing these spells she sought the seclusion of her new home, but now she felt compelled to be around other people. This was odd since Jill liked animals much better than people.

Jill thought to herself, *I've really got to get away for awhile. This trip will do me good.*

She decided to relax a little and watch the news while waiting on her shuttle to the airport.

"...Officials warn against traveling near Terminal Market as civil unrest continues. The Department of Transportation and Safety encourages all commuters to give themselves plenty of extra time traveling since traffic has been re-routed around the affected areas. Coming up, what is an epidemic and what can you do to protect yourself and your family? Next, on News at Eleven."

"Nothing but gloom and doom on the news," Jill said to the blank television screen.

She stood and began to pace back and forth when her ride to the airport arrived. Jill walked outside with her bags and met the driver. He was a short and stocky middle-aged fellow that wore a small, narrow-brimmed hat.

With a look of surprise, Jill told the man, "That was quick. I thought I'd be waiting for another half hour."

"Nah, I left early, didn't want to be late. All that mess goin' on downtown has traffic backed up across the Delaware."

"What's going on down there?"

"Where you been lady? Everybody's talkin' about it. Some kinda disease, epidemic, or somethin'. They got the whole place around Terminal blocked off..."

Almost immediately upon hearing the driver's voice, Jill felt the familiar flood of warmth and the tingling sensations fill her body. She felt her eyes getting heavy and had the unnatural compulsion to get close to him, to touch him, and to be touched by him.

"...Hey lady, you listenin' to what I'm sayin'? Get in the backseat! No one's allowed up front!"

Jill was horrified. Her mind was frantically trying to piece together what had just happened.

*What am I doing? What did he say to me? How long have I been sitting here?*

With all the dignity she could muster, Jill got in the backseat. She attempted to look demure and apologized.

"I'm so sorry. I'm just used to sitting up front and I instinctively got in on the passenger side. I've got this big meeting coming up and I was daydreaming. Please excuse me."

The driver looked at her suspiciously in the rearview mirror before saying, "Forget about it."

Jill was quiet for the rest of the drive to the airport.

She kept thinking, *What's happening to me? I really have to get out more.*

The warm tingling sensation had not gone away and she decided what she really needed was a man.

Thankfully, Jill's wait at the airport terminal was short. She was no longer anxious about the recent events of the day but was feeling very sleepy instead. She couldn't wait to get on the plane so she could rest. The next thing Jill knew she was walking down the articulated corridor connecting the airplane to the terminal with no memory of the last fifteen minutes. Jill didn't even know if she was boarding the right plane. She became very anxious again and was on the verge of panicking when she caught the scent of something heavenly, it was some sort of perfume she guessed. She began to tingle all over and suddenly felt very good and was no longer tired.

Jill was quite comfortable in her window seat, with the exception of an annoying biting fly that stowed away onboard. She was on the left-hand side and bottom floor of a double-decker behemoth, the A380-800 Airbus. The flight attendant was a bouncy brunette who seemed to hover around like a hummingbird waiting to sip nectar. Strangely, Jill found her very attractive and couldn't help thinking about her. She also couldn't help thinking about the businessman from Tokyo she was seated beside. He was a nice fellow and Jill thought he smelled good. Of course, there were the typical screaming children and their offensive parents who seemed oblivious to the screaming. Jill placed earplugs in her ears and drifted off to sleep while thinking about her trip.

Overall, it was a rather pleasant flight, up until they reached Australian airspace.

Jill awoke suddenly and felt very strange. Something was terribly wrong. Her heart was pounding irregularly. All the colors were wrong. What should've been red was now green and vice versa. Her eyes shot back and forth like someone deep in R.E.M sleep. The sounds of the airplane, the voice of the hummingbird-like flight attendant and the screaming of the children all dropped several octaves. It sounded horrible, wobbly and distorted as if she were hearing it all through a tin can underwater. The sounds in her head had become so loud she could hear nothing else. Images of everything she had ever seen or imagined were now replaying for her. Her eyes rolled back into her head until only the white parts showed. Large volumes of frothy saliva spilled uncontrollably from her now gaping mouth. She moaned softly at first and then all of her senses swirled together and merged in one final moment. Her body spasmed violently and she released her last guttural groan. Jill Sorensen was dead.

"Somebody help! This lady! I think she sick!" shouted the Japanese man sitting beside Jill.

The flight attendant rushed over to Jill who was now slumped over in his lap.

"Miss? Miss! Are you okay?"

Other than the whine of the airplane engines there was no sound on the lower deck of the airbus. All eyes were on the lifeless form of Jill Sorensen.

"She have medicral I.D. bracerat!" shouted the Japanese man.

The flight attendant raised Jill off the man's lap and tried to take her pulse. There was none. She radioed the Captain to tell him they had a medical emergency and then began C.P.R on Jill.

"...Eleven and; twelve and; thirteen and; fourteen and; fifteen and; check for breathing and a pulse," the attendant called out during chest compressions.

There was still no pulse so she began again. With amazing speed and ferocity, Jill grabbed the flight attendant's head in both of her hands and bit deeply into the side of her neck. The attendant let out a blood-curdling scream and pulled away as fast as she had been attacked. A fountain of blood splattered everyone within three seats of the spectacle as the flight attendant thrashed around in the isle. The bite would not have been as bad if the attendant hadn't pulled away. But this caused a huge plug of flesh to be ripped out of her neck, severing her carotid artery. Jill stood and spit the quivering chunk of flesh out of her mouth and it landed with a sickening splat. She was a horrible sight now. Her flesh was the color of a slug's underside. Bright red arterial-blood was smeared across her face and ran down her chin. All of the blood vessels in her neck and face were purple and stood in stark contrast to her dead flesh. The helpless flight attendant continued spluttering and gasping as Jill stepped over her. The brunette died within minutes.

Chaos ensued. Everyone ran screaming toward the front of the plane, trampling all who weren't able to move as quickly. Jill turned and grabbed the Japanese man who had been sitting beside her and bit into his arm. He pulled away and fell backward into an empty seat. A father who was now holding his child was attacked from behind. His wife snatched the child from his arms and ran to relative safety while the father turned and began pounding Jill with his fists. At 220 lbs., he packed quite a wallop but she just wouldn't go down. Repeatedly he punched Jill in the face, stomach, and ribs. The man drew back his right arm for the last time, winding-up for a massive punch when it happened. With lightening speed, Jill grabbed his left arm and bent the man's wrist downward at an impossible angle. A snapping sound could be heard over the man's screams. Just as quickly, she twisted his arm to the side, stuffed his open hand into her mouth, and chewed off some fingers. Streams of blood shot skyward from the stumps, spattering the ceiling, seats, and walls of the airplane.

Then out of nowhere; an air marshal appeared with his weapon drawn.

"Get down! Get down on the floor now! If you don't comply I will shoot you!"

The snarling corpse formerly known as Jill ran toward the air-marshal. He fired once into her chest sending bits of flesh and bone into the air behind her but it wasn't enough. Before he could fire, again she was on top of him, biting into his arm.

"Get off of me you crazy bitch!" he screamed.

He hit her in the middle of the face with his gun, shattering her nose and her front teeth. She made a deep gurgling sound and fell to the floor. As the man began to stand, Jill was on him again. This time she clamped down onto his nose with her remaining teeth and then pulled away slowly and deliberately. Blood spurted from the hole where the air marshal's nose had once been. He would save no one on this trip, not even himself.

Now that the air-marshal was down, Jill turned toward the other passengers of the plane. While her attention was focused elsewhere, the Japanese businessman knelt down and picked up the air marshal's gun. He stared at it briefly, unsure what to do with it. He then looked up at the screaming people huddled in the front of the plane. They were trying to escape the terror that had been unleashed upon them but there was nowhere to go. Eight hundred fifty-two people were stuck on an airplane with a zombie, 34,000 ft. above Australia. Jill started to move toward them when her forehead exploded in a loud *BANG*, spray-painting many of the passengers and part of the lower deck of the Airbus with blood and gore. She fell immediately to the floor. It was a macabre scene. The Japanese businessman was standing directly behind her crumpled body, his shaking hand still pointing the air-marshal's gun at the corpse. His eyes were wide with fright and his mouth was pulled tightly into a grimace. Gun-smoke and a fine mist of blood floated through the plane like cemetery fog.

The captain radioed their medical emergency to the tower and there were emergency personnel on the scene when the plane arrived. A host of physicians and law enforcement officers greeted the passengers, as they were off-loaded. It was terribly frightening even for a group of people that had just witnessed the brutal killing of fellow passengers. Security officials relentlessly interrogated every person who was on the plane and able to speak. Their accounts of what happened were as varied as their backgrounds. The Japanese businessman swore that a zombie had attacked the air-marshal, while a flight attendant claimed that it was definitely a terrorist that had killed the stewardess. Twenty-four hours later the Australian authorities released the passengers.

# RESCUE

**November 28**
**Center City:**

Jake knelt on the sidewalk in front of the liquor store, grieving over Heather's lifeless body. Carl was leaning against the building and looking the other direction while cradling his mangled left arm with his good hand.

"In case anyone was wondering, I've been shot and I need help," Jameson said sarcastically.

"You son of a bitch!" Shams said with a thick Bengali accent. "I can't believe your insensitivity! A person has just passed away and all you can think of is yourself!"

"Hey I'm bleeding okay and it hurts like hell!"

Shams kicked Jameson in the right leg where he had been shot.

"Arghhhh, you asshole! Ohh! We're all going to die," Jameson moaned and began to cry.

"Big baby," Shams said while shaking his head and turning away.

Bill had waited as long as he dared.

"Jake, man I'm so sorry. I wish I could've helped. She's gone brother. I wanted to give you a minute alone but we've got trouble commin' up the street, if you know what I mean."

Jake stood and began walking briskly toward the dead shopkeeper. He bent down, took the gun from the man, and turned it over in his own hand while staring at it.

Bill was clearly worried.

"Hey man you okay?"

As he looked back at his dead ex-wife Jake replied in a frighteningly dead-pan voice, "Let's move Bill. Carl you coming?"

Carl simply nodded.

There are no words that could express the pain, guilt, and anger Jake was feeling. All of his emotions coalesced into rage, allowing no room for fear.

The group was already past the shop-keeper when they heard Jameson shouting at them.

"Hey, I can't walk! You guys have to help me! You can't leave me here! Hey!"

Jake turned around and pointed his gun at Jameson. He considered shooting him. He needed to kill something, take something away as Heather was taken from him.

Jameson cried out, "Wait! Stop! What are you doing man? Don't do this! I didn't kill her! It's not my fault! Don't kill me please!"

"You can drag your sorry ass along behind us," Jake said in that same dead-pan voice.

He then turned and continued jogging. The rest of the crew began following him, not knowing what else to do. Jameson pulled himself to his feet and began limping after the rapidly departing crew. There were droves of zombies shambling up the street behind him. Jameson kept looking back and crying like a child. They were leaving him.

"We can't just leave him back there," Sue admonished Jake.

Jake turned toward the pitiful figure of Jameson who was hobbling along and sniffling like a child. Jake lifted the pistol he had taken from the storeowner and pointed it at Jameson.

Looking up, Jameson shouted, "Jesus, no!"

"Get out of the way damn it!" Jake shouted impatiently.

Jameson hobbled off to one side and Jake fired at the first zombie leading the pack. It was a nice shot.

"Hurry up Jameson! I don't have all day here!"

Jake fired again, and again, each time taking careful aim and pulling the trigger with a fluid motion. Jake, who was now sweating profusely, noticed after the first zombie had fallen that there were several using the others as shields.

*My God... intelligence, some of these things are smart!* he thought.

"Jameson move your ass!"

"I'm trying!"

Then there was a crackling sound all around them and Jake had the distinct feeling that a warm wind had suddenly passed by. All the creatures were down. Jake turned around to see Bill standing there with the E.M.P. weapon balanced on his hip.

"Damn thing worked Doc," Bill said with a grin.

"Yes, but they won't stay down forever. We need to go now. Hurry up Jameson!"

Jake met Jameson halfway and allowed him to lean on his shoulder. They constantly glanced back down the street as they jogged toward the University. The zombies were getting back up.

"They're coming! Keep moving everyone!" Jake called out.

Ahead of them they could see the blinking lights of a police barricade.

"Up there! I think we'll be alright if we get to the barricade!" shouted Bill.

"There's no time! Hit them with the gun again Bill!" commanded Jake.

Bill stopped jogging and wheeled around, aiming the gun at the approaching horde. Jake had stopped too and was watching with interest, his gun at the ready. For a second time, Jake saw the two zombies using the others as shields. Jake was ready. As soon as Bill fired his weapon, he would shoot them. Without warning most of the zombies fell to the ground.

*Bill must have fired,* thought Jake.

But before he could get off a clean shot the two he was after dove into buildings on opposite sides of the street.

"Did you see that Doc? Some of them damn things can think!" Bill said with awe.

"Yeah I thought that's what I saw earlier, only I wasn't sure until now."

"You wanna go after 'em?" Bill asked, looking eager for a fight.

"No! We need to keep moving. We have to catch up to the others if we want them to make it to the barricade. Shams looked like he was having a hell of a time with Carl hanging on him. He's gonna need some help… and they'll need our firepower," Jake said while breathing heavily.

"Hey! Up here! My wife and I are trapped! Help us…please!" one panicked and lonely voice pleaded from the third floor of a building directly above the street where the zombies lay motionless.

Jake's expression was one of anger and determination. He looked up the street toward the barricade and then back up at the building where the cries of help had emanated.

Bill saw the look on Jake's face and knew what he was about to do.

"Aw hell Jake you can't go in there alone! Let's do it together. I'll watch your back."

"I won't be long. Take Jameson, catch up with the others and hurry! They need your help up there."

"We need you too man! What good is it to get to the University if you're dead? None of us knows what to do once we get there." Bill tried reasoning with Jake but he wouldn't budge.

Jake smiled and said reassuringly to Bill, "I don't plan on getting killed my friend. I'll see you guys in a minute now get going."

"Fine, one last thing," Bill raised his gun and aimed it toward Jake.

Northrop ducked and heard the crackling sound and felt the sensation of a warm breeze passing. He looked down the street, where he would be going in a few moments, to see the dead crumple to the ground.

"Saved my ass again Bill."

"Yeah and you owe me brother!" Bill said with a grin.

He then turned and started toward the barricade. Jake took one last look at Bill and Jameson jogging up the street and then ran in the opposite direction. He suddenly felt very alone and began to wonder if he had made the right decision.

*No going back now,* he thought.

He briefly considered shooting the stunned corpses in the head when he got to them but decided against slowing down. At the moment he reached them, the emergency warning sirens began to wail.

"Oh super!" Jake shouted at the sky while trying to hold his hands over his ears.

Apparently, there was a siren mounted very close by. The sound was both dreadful and deafening. Jake made it to the building's entrance and noticed the front door was smashed. It didn't look like a retail store. It looked more like an office building. The lights were out in the front so he couldn't see the name. In fact, he just now realized the lights were out all around town. He hadn't counted on this. For the first time since Heather had died, Jake was scared.

*Oh shit. Don't panic Jake. Think damn it,* he said to himself.

Emergency lights began blinking on in buildings all around him but the entrance directly in front of Jake was still pitch black.

*Come on damn it, turn on!*

He fought the urge to run back up the street toward the barricades and safety.

Then, with a tiny flicker, the entrance now had its own emergency light. It really was a tiny light but anything was better than the inky blackness that might be hiding the stuff of nightmares.

Jake moved slowly into the building, not knowing what to expect. The words of the man yelling out of the third floor window replayed in his mind. *...My wife and I are trapped...* Jake thought about the scared man's words and hoped it wasn't the dead that had them trapped. He didn't have the luxury of ignorance for very long. He caught the smell of something dead and figured one or more of those things were near. Jake desperately wished the sirens would stop wailing. He'd never be able to hear something or someone closing in on him until it was too late. Jake was now deep in the lobby of the building. He judged that it was probably a law firm based on the ornate furniture and the bookshelves lined with thick books. It was too dark to tell what was written on them. There were only two emergency lights in the lobby and one was already well behind him. As he approached the second light, the dead-smell became stronger. Mercifully, the sirens began to fall silent. Jake's ears strained to pick up any indication of movement around him, while the last remnants of the wailing sirens faded.

The lobby became as quiet as a crypt. The only thing Jake could hear was the blood pounding in his ears and his own breathing. His hands were sweaty and his mouth had gone dry. He stood motionless for several minutes as he tried to formulate a plan. In the distance, he began to hear the low murmuring of voices. His stomach tightened as he listened. Jake started to move toward the sounds taking great care to make as little noise as possible. With each step, Jake winced and imagined it sounded like a book slamming shut. After a few paces, he stopped and looked down while shaking his head.

*What are you doing Jake? Get it together. Come on, focus,* Jake silently admonished himself.

He took in a great big breath and exhaled slowly while closing his eyes. Swallowing hard he opened them and once more began moving toward the voices. Jake paused after every few steps to listen. The voices were growing louder but something wasn't right. Whoever was speaking seemed to be mumbling constantly and incoherently. He still couldn't make out anything they were saying, after walking closer to the sounds. Jake's imagination had free reign now. All manner of horrors were just out of sight. His eyes darted wildly back and forth searching for a way out of his current situation. Just then he saw the dim, green glow of a sign peeking around the bend.

*Stairs!* Jake shouted in his mind as he craned his neck to see the stairwell sign.

It was in the same direction from which the voices were emanating. There didn't seem to be anything between Jake and the corridor leading to the stairs. Jake moved deliberately forward with his back against the wall and his gun outstretched in front of him. The dim emergency light barely made it around the bend in the corridor. Oddly, Jake saw faint lines of light playing on the wall to his left. He rounded the bend to find that the corridor opened into a cavernous room and the sounds he had been hearing were suddenly louder. He spun to his right and discovered the source of the phantom voices haunting his every move. Water was babbling through a faux tropical setting in a huge, lighted wall-fountain. For whatever reason, the designers of this building had wired the wall-display into the emergency power. The trickling of running water in the fountain had become the voices of the dead. His imagination had gotten the best of him.

Jake's heart was pounding so hard that it rebounded painfully off his ribcage. He leaned over and put his hands on his knees, while breathing a sigh of relief. When Jake stood upright, again he smelled the foul stench of death. Relief turned to fear as he struggled to see into the darkness in front of him. The weak, greenish-colored light from the fountain made everything appear to move. In this watery light, Jake could see a retaining wall filled with an assortment of tall plants about thirty feet away. Anything beyond that was cloaked in darkness. Jake's stairwell sign appeared to float in midair on the other side of the retaining wall. He hugged the right-hand side of the room as he maneuvered around the wall-fountain. As he edged closer to the retaining wall, Jake could see that there were two floors, the higher one he was standing on and a lower level on the other side of the wall. The odor of putrid flesh was overpowering now, forcing Jake to blink hard several times while trying not to gag. He heard the sounds of shuffling feet and froze.

"Oh God," Jake whispered to himself as he stared at the parade of dead milling around beneath the sign.

It was too dark to get an accurate count of the rotting creatures below him but there were far more of them than there were bullets in his gun. Jake had no choice. He turned slowly and retreated through the lobby. He nearly tripped on a broken coat rack lying in the middle of the floor. It was an oddly designed piece of furniture with a series of metal poles joined at the top. A weld had broken and one of the heavy poles was now loose. He decided it may prove useful and carefully pried it free of the rack.

Jake silently proceeded to the entrance of the building. He told himself that the people on the third floor were safe so long as they stayed put. He peered out into the street to see if the stunned corpses were still there. They weren't. He could hear gunfire in the distance and wondered if Bill and the others were all right. He stood at the entrance, wrestling with his conscience when an unexpected image flashed into his mind. It was Carl covered in putrid human remains. Jake then remembered the two zombies that had used their dim-witted brethren as shields.

*That's it! They're selfish like us! That means they can't have a collective consciousness! I can mask my scent and slip past those things!* Thought Jake.

Now all he had to do was find a corpse that *wasn't* moving. As soon as he had the thought, a man's weak voice called out from the lobby making Jake jump.

"Missssterrr," slurred the thin voice was that was both wet and raspy.

Jake whirled around and stepped backward onto the street with his gun raised. He could see a figure approaching but couldn't tell if it was human.

"Who are you?"

The reply that came was a throaty, hissing noise.

"You gotta be kidding me," Jake quietly said to himself.

Not wanting to draw the attention of revenants, he put the gun in his waistband and then with both hands lifted the heavy metal pole he had been carrying. Without warning, something charged at him with frightening speed. Jake wasn't ready. He swung at its head but missed, hitting instead its shoulder. There was a wet thud and then it toppled over sideways. Jake didn't wait for it to get back up. He swung the pole repeatedly at the rotting thing, hitting it in the upper back and neck. The wet cracking sounds, as the pole connected with the zombie, reminded Jake of hitting raw eggs with an aluminum baseball bat. Jake pounded the thing mercilessly but the angle wasn't right and he couldn't get in any shots to its head. With a sickening crunch, Jake finally brought the pole down on the base of its skull, spattering the sidewalk with putrid green slime. Breathing hard, Jake dropped to his knees and let the pole slip from his hands. His mind was racing. Had the thing really spoken to him or was it just his imagination? Jake couldn't decide but was terrified by the thought of it.

Jake knelt over the dead man and then began to heave because of the smell. He stood quickly, turned his back to the corpse, and puked onto the concrete. Jake questioned his resolve.

"Jesus Christ, I don't think I can do this," he said to himself.

He thought about Heather and the horrible manner in which she had died. The way she had looked to Jake for help, her eyes pleading with him to save her. Jake's eyes filled with water as he gritted his teeth together.

"No! No one else will die because of me!" he said through clenched teeth.

Jake knelt down and faced the corpse again. This time he thrust his hand deeply into its open skull and then struggled to pull out a handful of putrescence. Jake was puzzled by this resistance. The contents of the skull were being held in place by some sort of connective tissue resembling the innards of a pumpkin.

"What the hell is this?" Jake asked himself as he pulled the stringy mess loose of the skull. "This crap is tough. Is this..? It can't be," Jake said aloud, remembering the spider-silk genes he inserted into *Geobacter*.

There was no time to ponder the implications of his discovery. He smeared the decaying matter over his arms and chest, vomiting repeatedly. He thrust his hand back into the corpse a second and then a third time, ripping out dripping handfuls of decomposing filth and rubbing it all over his entire body. Jake then filled his pockets with as much of the fetid corpse as he could carry. He had a plan.

Jake walked back through the lobby of the building without any attempt at stealth. Once again, he was in the cavernous room where the sign floated in midair. Instead of hugging the wall as he had done earlier, Jake walked straight for the stairs leading to the lower floor. The wall-fountain provided the only weak illumination in the room. He paused briefly at the top of the stairs as he looked down upon the throngs of dead and was glad he couldn't see them clearly. He mimicked their movements as he lumbered down each step. Most of the dead were stumbling around growling, moaning, and wheezing. They seem to take little notice of him as he walked through their ranks. Jake thought he had nothing left in his stomach to disgorge but the fetor of so many rotting corpses proved him wrong. Without trying to hide it, Jake simply opened his mouth and spewed as he continued to shuffle along. He noticed a few of the dead had stopped moving and had turned to face him. Jake continued toward the stairs. He could see the elevators and the door to the stairwell. Waves of nausea were hitting him like punches from a prizefighter. He spewed again and this time he heard the shuffling behind him grow quiet. He bolted toward the door to the stairs without looking back. Jake slammed into the door and fell through onto the floor as it swung open. He kicked it shut and then used the metal pole from the coat rack to brace the door so the zombies couldn't get in. They were banging on the door and the sounds of their frustrated attempts reverberated inside the stairwell.

Jake wasted no time getting up the stairs. The emergency lighting was well placed allowing him to run at full speed. He knew those things might break through his hastily constructed barrier at any moment. Cautiously, he approached the door to the third floor while brandishing his gun. Jake gave himself the mental okay and pushed it open. Thankfully, there was nothing on the other side waiting to attack. The third floor appeared relatively unscathed to Jake as he surveyed his new surroundings. Knowing his appearance was hideous and not wanting to frighten the trapped people, he announced his presence.

"Hello! Anybody here? I'm the man who was outside on the street a little while ago! You called down to me for help! I know I look frightening but I had to disguise myself to get in here! Hello!"

A visibly shaken man wearing a white button-down shirt and khaki pants stepped out from behind a cubicle and shouted, "Stay there! Don't come any closer! I have a gun!"

"Easy now, you asked me for help and I'm here to do what I can for you and your wife," Jake said reassuringly.

"My name is Jake Northrop. I am a professor over at the University. What's your name?"

The man was trying not to cry but he kept grimacing.

With a pained expression on his face, he answered in a wavering voice, "How do I know I can trust you?"

He kept peering back over his left shoulder at something only he could see. He shook his head and lowered his gun. "I'm Chris Kelly. I work here."

"Good to meet you Mr. Kelly. Is your wife okay?"

Chris looked over his shoulder again and said, "I don't know."

"Where is she Mr. Kelly? We have to get out of here right now."

"Brandi's sick."

Jake fought to keep his composure, "Chris please— where is Brandi?"

"She's in the bathroom."

"Alright then let's go and get…"

Abruptly Chris stopped Jake before he could finish his sentence, "No I'll go! You stay here!"

"Chris I know you've been through a lot but you have to trust me okay."

Chris was still staring over his shoulder without talking. Jake knew he had to concede.

"Look I'll go with you to the door and then you can go in alone. I'll be right outside if you need any help. From now on, we do everything together. We don't want to get separated once we get down there," Jake said while nodding toward the stairwell.

Chris reluctantly agreed at last.

Jake waited outside the women's bathroom while Chris went inside to get his wife. He listened intently for any signs of trouble and was becoming impatient at having to wait for them. He thought he heard Chris crying and decided to give him another moment when he heard a throaty hissing noise coming from the bathroom. Jake's heart nearly stopped. He'd heard the same sound in the lobby. He gently opened the bathroom door and was greeted by the horrible stench of vomit and human excrement. He could smell it over the putrid goop that was smeared all over his own body. Chris was kneeling down in front of his wife who was slowly and unnaturally squirming her way toward him.

"Brandi what's wrong with you? Say something," moaned Chris.

She released another blood-curdling hissing noise, like a prolonged death rattle.

"Chris, get away from it now! That's not your wife anymore!"

"Get out of here! Leave us alone!"

"I'm sorry man but she's gone. That thing in front of you isn't your wife. It's just an empty shell like those things down in the lobby and it will kill you."

"You're crazy! Look she needs my help."

"Chris, listen to me. How long ago was she bitten, two weeks ago, three maybe?"

"How do you know about that?"

"That doesn't matter now. What matters is that you understand what's happened here."

"It does matter! Is that why she's sick?"

"Look we're running out of time here!"

"Leave goddamn it!"

Jake shook his head and said with resignation, "Fine, I've seen it happen before. I watched an old lady who had been bitten die and come back as one of those things. She became a mindless machine bent on infecting others or worse."

"How can she be…you said the old lady came back so there's still a chance. I mean if I get her to a hospital…"

"You aren't listening to me! She's dead! That thing in front of you is no longer your wife. It's not even human!"

"I can't leave her here, not like this," Chris sobbed.

Jake understood all too well the pain Chris was feeling.

"Chris you have some choices to make and none of them are pleasant. You can leave this thing here and come with me, you can stay here and let it kill you, or if you can't stand to leave it here you can kill it and then we can leave. But you think about this: you asked for my help and I risked my life and the life of the others I was helping to come and rescue you and your wife. Sadly, nobody can help your wife. She's gone but you're alive. Do you think she would want you to die at the hands of this thing impersonating her? No, she'd want you to live. Do it for her even if you can't do it for yourself."

Chris was torn. His whole world had just ended and he didn't know what to do. He looked at the thing inching its way toward him and then up at Jake.

"I'll go..." he began to say but the rest was obliterated by a sudden *bang* as Jake raised his gun and fired.

The lifeless form of Brandi Kelly fell heavily onto her husband. He lay there clutching her in his arms while crying pitifully. Jake reached down and took Chris' gun in case he thought of doing something stupid.

"I'll be outside. We only have a couple of minutes."

Chris came out a little while later looking drained and rather pale. Jake told him he was sorry for his loss and explained that he had just lost someone too. As they walked toward the stairwell, Jake again asked Chris how long it had been since his wife was bitten. Chris dropped a bombshell on the professor.

"We were attacked by our next-door neighbor about four days ago. He bit her while they were arguing over a friggin' trashcan that our dog knocked over. I tried to break it up and he got me too. He's always been weird but he just seemed...I don't know... not the same. Anyway, a day or so after that we both got sick. I just had a fever. I got better but she just kept getting worse. I told her not to come to work today but she was afraid of losing her job and..."

Chris lost his composure and started crying again.

"I'm sorry Chris; did you say four days ago?"

Sniffling he said, "Yeah why?"

"That's not possible."

"What's not possible?" Chris said, coming out of his reverie.

"There's no time for me to explain now. We need to get out of here. Are you sure there's no one else in the building...ehem, alive?"

"Nobody, all the others went home early to beat the traffic and I...we stayed to catch up on some work."

Chris had made a great effort to include his late wife when he spoke. He was trying to keep her alive and in the present rather than only alive in his memory. Jake needed Chris here with him. He knew he had to do something.

"Here smell this," Jake said.

"What is it?"

Chris took the handful of goop from Jake and brought it up to his nose. He turned his head and immediately puked.

"Oh my God that's disgusting! Why'd you do that to me?"

"You have to smear this all over you. I know it stinks but it's our only hope of getting out of here alive."

"No way! I can't... blughhh!" with that he puked again.

"Best to get all that out now," Jake said while patting Chris on the back.

"You don't want to be doing that while you're pretending to be a zombie, now do you?"

When they arrived at the ground floor, it was quiet. Jake discovered that his metal brace had held. He pressed his ear up to the door for a few seconds and then nodded.

"Yep, they're still out there alright."

"Where'd they all come from?" whispered Chris.

"Most of them were probably indigents."

"There's so many. Why didn't anybody notice something was wrong?"

"Because they're homeless and nobody gives a shit if they're sick or not. We can talk about it later but right now we have more important things to do. Remember, once you get to the steps start running and don't stop even when you've made it outside. Are you ready?"

"No," Chris shook his head.

"I'm gonna be sick again."

"Puke quietly now. Those things can hear."

Chris heaved almost silently into his own shirt. As sorry as Jake felt for Chris he couldn't help chuckling a little. The good professor was indeed a strange man.

"Do you need some more time?" Jake asked, suppressing a grin.

"No. Let's do this," Chris said as he wiped his mouth on his shoulder.

"Oh God I forgot it's on my shoulder too."

Jake shook his head and chuckled some more at the pitiful site of Chris Kelly spitting out the filth that covered them both. Jake knew Chris was already infected so it really didn't matter that he had gotten it in his mouth. In fact, if Jake couldn't find a cure for *Zombacter* Chris would most likely end up just like his wife Brandi, they all might.

Completely sober now, Jake once again asked Chris if he was ready. Chris nodded and Jake quietly removed the metal pole and slowly opened the door. It was much darker in the room than Jake remembered. He bumped into one of them after only a few steps but continued his shuffling until he reached the stairs. He took one look back to make sure Chris was still behind him and then sprinted up the stairs and out into the lobby. Chris was right on his heels. Jake tripped as he passed through the entrance of the building sending both of them crashing into a heap on the sidewalk.

"Get up! Go! Go! Go!" Chris shouted.

Jake made it to his feet and started after Chris who was already well ahead of him.

"Run toward that flashing light and don't stop for anything!" Jake yelled to Chris. He chanced a quick look over his shoulder and saw dark forms pouring out of the entrance to the building like angry ants from a mound that had just been kicked. A cramp in Jake's side threatened to slow him down but he continued to run. He thought for sure that his muscles were cramping hard enough to tear his side apart.

*Jesus, I didn't think the barricade was that far away!* Jake thought to himself after running for several minutes.

It was a long run indeed. Jake was seeing a barricade in front of the Schuykill Bridge bordering Center City. Walnut was a straight street after all and the flashing lights could be seen from over a mile away. Jake's lungs were burning badly now and his legs were so heavy he was having trouble lifting them. He was out of shape and slowing down. Up ahead he could see that the barricade was in front of the bridge and there were other people milling about, at least he hoped they were people. He was afraid to look back so he kept running; jogging was more like it. As slow as he was moving he still caught up to Chris who was obviously in distress.

"Almost …there!" huffing and puffing, Jake encouraged Chris.

Chris stared straight ahead, gasped for air, and looked very wobbly.

Just then, Jake heard noises behind them and looked back. There were dozens of the dead racing toward them at a much greater speed than Jake and Chris were moving. They were so close; if he had a stone, he could've hit one of them with it.

"Hey! Up there! Help! They're coming!" Jake managed to shout between great big breaths.

Jake felt a warm breeze pass and had an odd prickling sensation all over his skin.

*Bill!* Jake felt a small burst of energy and grabbed Chris by the arm to help him get to the barricade.

"Good to see you again Doc! Thought I was gonna have to come get you!" shouted a grinning Bill.

Jake couldn't think of a time in his life when he was happier to see someone except maybe the last time Bill had saved him.

"Picked up a couple more people and some weapons on the way. Are you okay to shoot?" Bill asked

"Yeah," Jake said breathing heavily.

"Good, I've got somthin' for you."

Bill thrust an M16 into Jake's hands.

"Got a full clip in her. Battery don't have much juice though. We've been usin' 'em pretty heavy since you left. We're all armed now. Got plenty of clips so let her rip. Got somethin' else too, here body armor. This stuff is light as a feather and tough as hell. Watch this." Bill held the thin black material down with one foot and stabbed at it with his knife.

"Nothin' not a scratch."

"I don't think they're going to be shooting at us Bill. Besides, it's too hot. Why don't you wear it?" Jake said between great big breaths of air.

"Suit yourself, Doc. You ready?"

"Yeah just give me a few seconds to catch my breath."

Bill propped the gun upon his stump of an arm before saying, "Take as long as you want Doc. Looks like you got about five seconds before all hell's gonna break loose."

"Aww shit!"

“Aim at their heads! Stun ‘em and gun’em boys! Whoooohoooo!” Bill let out a war cry and then the shooting began.

It was a fierce battle. At first, the only ones who were able to shoot straight were Bill, Jake, and Shams. Bullets were tearing into the rotting corpses but few were headshots. Each time someone fired an E.M.P. it took thirty seconds or longer to recharge and it always seemed that more zombies were running up to take the places of those that fell while many more could be seen shambling along in the distance. Once the corpses had fallen, Jake’s team usually had to wait until the dead started to get back up before they could make a clean kill; meanwhile new zombies would close in requiring all of their attention. Some of the revenants were screaming as they leapt inhuman distances to land right in front of the barricade.

With all of their practice, most of the other crewmembers were getting much better with their aim. Mary was becoming a respectable marksman and at least Jameson was holding his own now. Bill was so skilled that he made death dealing seem effortless. Jake fired each shot with a fluid motion and nearly every one hit its mark. His years of practice with the Philadelphia marksmanship team as a youth was serving him well. Carl was having a lot more difficulty than the others were because of his injuries. His morphine had worn off, he was in a great deal of pain, and yet he fought on. Shams had to keep reloading the gun for Carl but he was a decent shot.

“Die you bastards!” Sue screamed as she unloaded into the forehead of yet another zombie.

“Clip!” she screamed.

Jameson tossed her the clip but it over-shot Sue’s hand, hit a corpse in the face instead, and then skidded across the road beyond the barricade.

Jake shot it cleanly through the skull with only inches to spare between the thing and Sue.

“Here you go!” Chris said while tossing another clip to Sue.

“Keep it up fellows we got ‘em on the run!” Bill shouted.

A zombie breached the barricade from the left and was almost on top of Bill when Chris shot it in midair. Everybody was being covered with bits of rotting flesh. The zombies were everywhere now. They just kept coming. Jake and the survivors were barely holding their ground when things suddenly got much worse. The dead began coming at them from all sides. Several came from behind them and Sue panicked. She turned and sent bullets whizzing past Shams and Jameson. A ghoul grabbed her arm but she continued firing as she fell backward, spraying bullets at her team, killing its two newest members. She was pleading with Bill to help her.

"Ahh! God no! Help me! Don't let them take me! No! Bill!"

Although he tried valiantly, Bill could do nothing to help. With a terrible strangled gurgle, her screams were gone. During the ensuing confusion, the dead gained the advantage. The barricade was overrun and the crew was forced to flee toward the bridge. Just when Jake thought they weren't going to make it, a huge explosion knocked him off his feet. When Jake stood he couldn't see the dead any more through the dust and smoke billowing up from where the barricade had been. Bits and pieces of rotting flesh and concrete still rained down. Coughing and spitting, Jake wiped at his eyes, then plugged one nostril while forcing air out the other, and then repeated the procedure for the other side.

"What the hell was that?" Jake inquired.

"Grenade, a little somthin' I picked up on the way! I don't think it got all of 'em and that's all I had! Where the hell'd you learn to shoot like that anyway?" asked Bill.

"Boy Scouts."

Bill arched his eyebrows and nodded approvingly.

Jake turned toward the rest of the group, "Look, is everybody okay? Yes, no? We don't have much time. Get up! We have to keep moving!"

The stunned yet alive group made their way across the bridge. Luckily there were far fewer creatures in front of them than there had been behind. For Jake, hours had passed since he and Chris made it to the barricade. Truly it had been less than fifteen minutes and in that time they had taken several casualties. Sue was gone, and so were the two newest members of the team. Jake never had the chance to thank them for their help much less learn their names.

Carl wasn't doing so well either. It was a scene reminiscent of the crucifixion; one of Carl's arms was slung over Bill's back and the other over Jake's back. The two were practically dragging him as they moved slowly toward the campus. Carl's head hung limp and occasionally he would moan, "Daddy's gonna make it honey".

Jake stared into the night but Bill would look at Carl and shake his head a little every time he moaned. Carl then grabbed Jake's shoulder surprisingly hard for someone on the verge of death, startling Jake.

"Heather's gone," Tears rolled down his face.

All three stopped in the middle of the road as Jake and Bill looked at each other and then at Carl.

"I have to be with my little girl. Help me get to my daughter. I can't leave her alone! She's all I ..." Carl's head fell once again against his chest.

"Is he…okay?" Mary inquired.

"No, but he's alive" Jake answered.

"Guys, you need to rest. Jameson and I can help Carl for a while okay?" Shams offered.

Jameson looked very surprised when Shams offered his services without consulting him first. Amazingly, whatever he was thinking he kept it to himself.

Bill continued walking alongside Jake so he could speak without the others hearing him

"Doc, he don't look so good. I don't think he's gonna make it much longer."

Jake looked back at Carl before answering, "Yeah, I think you're right. Once we're at the lab we'll make him as comfortable as possible. I have a few ideas I'd like to try. I might buy him some time."

Jake seemed to struggle with something a moment before saying to Bill, "I didn't know he had a daughter. Maybe he was just hallucinating."

"No Doc. That man has a family. I seen it in his eyes."

"How can you be so sure?"

"I had a family once…I just know that look."

As they neared the University, they encountered fewer and fewer reanimated corpses. The lights were still on around campus and aside from a total lack of people; there were few signs of disaster. Though they were exhausted the haggard group trudged on, each lost in their own reverie.

*I wonder if anybody's still here. God I hope they were evacuated out of the city. On second thought maybe not, nobody should leave. There's no telling who's infected. The whole city is probably quarantined and if it's not it sure as hell should be,* Jake decided as he pondered the idea of a city sterilized by the military.

They were almost to the lab now and he felt stabs of fear and excitement at the thought of being there again. For once in his life, Jake was glad to be in the company of other people. He'd always preferred to work alone but the events of tonight had proven that his life depended on other people. Thunder boomed ominously in the distance and a gentle breeze began to stir as they reached the entrance to the lab. Changes were coming and Jake Northrop would be in the center of them.

# REVENGE

**November 28:**

Jameson's argumentative nature re-emerged shortly before the group reached the Bioengineering building. It was fueled in part by the constant attacks from mosquitoes and biting flies.

"Where are all these bugs coming from? Did you screw up and make those too?" Jameson quipped.

Jake just ignored Jameson. After the last few heated exchanges, Jake decided it was pointless to be drawn into another debate.

"My freakin' leg's killing me and nobody cares. I can barely walk but I'm the one Zombie-boy's leaning on. None of this would've happened if he didn't try and screw around with nature," Jameson said to Shams while jutting his chin toward Jake. Jake breathed in deeply and then sighed. Shams stepped in front of Jameson, who was now the only person supporting Carl, and poked him in the chest with his finger.

"He saved your ass!"

"He's the one who got me...all of us into this mess! This is all his fault!"

"All you do is complain… about everything! Look at your leg, it's just a scratch! We are all tired of hearing about your problems! You are not the only one experiencing discomfort!" Shams articulately admonished Jameson in a heavy Bengali accent.

Carl raised his head briefly and slurred, "Both of you shut up. Man can't even…hear himself…" before he began mumbling incoherently.

Jake reached the side entrance to the building and noticed it was unlocked. Bill was behind the still arguing pair but wasn't listening to them. His attention was focused on Jake.

"Hey you two, be quiet for a minute!"

"He's the one who started this! If he pokes me in the chest one more time…"

Bill moved up beside Jameson and pressed a serrated hunting knife into his throat. The army vet whispered something into Jameson's ear only he could hear. All of the color drained from Jameson's face. Just as quickly as it happened, Bill's knife disappeared somewhere beneath his clothing. Bill looked completely innocent when Jake looked back at him.

"I think we have a problem. This door should've been locked."

"Well at least we know it ain't a zombie that done it."

Jake nodded.

"In any case, stay alert."

"You think them things mighta gotten in Doc?"

"Maybe, but don't just shoot anything you see. Remember, my students may be here. And listen, after we have a look around I'll need to get in touch with the CDC and whoever is running the show outside of town. That means I'm going to need everybody's cooperation. No more bickering. I think the phone lines are still working and the internet is up so we're in good shape for now."

"You gonna tell 'em what you know 'bout those things Doc?"

"It'd be a sin if I didn't."

The group walked cautiously through the door and entered the science building. It was eerily quiet inside.

"Hello, anybody here?"

"Shut up Jameson! Those things might be in here. Do you want them to know we're here?" admonished Shams.

"Look, if they are in here then we're gonna find out sooner or later. I'd prefer to know sooner if you get my drift. Besides, Doc said some of his kids might be here so it's probably not a bad idea if we let 'em know we're commin'," replied Bill.

"Quiet, I thought I heard something."

The silence stretched on for several moments before Bill eased alongside Jake.

"What'd ya hear Doc?" whispered Bill.

"I don't know. It sounded like a door closing. Let's take this one floor at a time, door by door and search this whole building.

My lab's on the lowest level so we'll need to go down one floor and work our way up."

"I thought we were on the lowest floor," Mary stated.

"No, this building was built into the side of a little hill so the second floor is level with the street."

"Oh."

"You guys sit tight for a minute while I check out this room."

"You got it Doc."

Jake disappeared into the nearest room and re-emerged a short time later.

"It's clear. Chris, if you don't mind will you stay here with Carl? It's a good spot for now."

Lightning flashed through the window and illuminated Chris' apprehensive looking face.

"Sure, I don't mind."

"When we're finished searching the building we'll all meet back here. Do you have a phone?"

"Yeah, why?"

Jake scribbled something on the back of a business card and handed it to Chris. "Here's my number. If you see or hear anything, call me. Keep trying to reach people, anyone that can help. Try the internet, post on Facebook, Twitter, anything…just try to get someone's attention."

After exchanging numbers, Chris took Carl into the classroom and locked the doors behind them.

"How about you Shams, do you have a phone?"

"Yes but sadly the battery isn't charged."

"Anybody else have a phone, Jameson?"

"What?"

Jake lifted his heavy eyebrows, took a deep breath, and turned to face Jameson. He spoke the words slowly and clearly, "A phone, do you have a phone?"

Jameson patted his pockets in an exaggerated manner while feigning a look of surprise and then smirked, "Nope, all outta phones here."

Jake looked down at the floor a moment before shaking his head and turning his back to Jameson.

"Alright then, let's go down to the lowest level and work our way up."

"Dr. Northrop, what about the stairs?"

"What about them Shams?"

"What if those things get in and come down the steps right after we have cleared a level?"

Jake and Bill looked at each other for a second before turning to Shams. It was Bill who spoke first.

"You gotta point there. Where'd you say you're from?"

"I am from Bangladesh. I work at…"

"Shams is right. We should secure all the entrances to the building before we go any further. We'll do this together; to make sure nobody gets into trouble. We'll start with the door we came through and lock 'em all down. After that, we'll put a person in each stairwell and work our way up as we search the floors," Jake explained.

Securing the doors proved to be an easy task. All were locked with the exception of the one they originally entered on the right side. Keeping them secured was another problem altogether. The entire front of the building was made of glass. Mary was the first to point out this obvious flaw in their plans.

"We'll hear if someone breaks the glass getting in. Besides it's the best we can do right now."

Jake was relieved that Jameson wasn't trying to stir-up trouble again. Maybe whatever Bill said to him earlier did some good. Even so, Jake was suspicious of his motives.

"Alright, now we can search the building. Everybody ready?"

Several people nodded distractedly while rain pelted the glass and thunder shook the widows in their casings. Jake took one last look outside before walking toward the stairs. The group followed him and began their descent to the lowest level. Halfway down the stairs they began finding blood smeared on the walls and floor. There were distinct sneaker and handprints on the stairs heading back up to the floor they just left.

"This ain't good Doc."

Jake Northrop remained silent but inside he was burning with guilt and fear.

*Not the kids... please not the kids,* he kept repeating over and over in his mind, hoping that fate may see fit to spare him from this nightmare.

They moved slowly and deliberately down the steps.

"Careful, keep your guard up we know them things was here," cautioned Bill.

A pale light was flickering over the landing to the lowest floor; dimly illuminating a figure slumped in the corner. Blood and gore was everywhere. The search party stopped and stared at the broken body before them.

"Doc, is it...do you know who it is?"

The body was so badly mangled that he couldn't identify it from where he stood transfixed. Jake's insides were bound in a dreadful knot. Haltingly, his legs carried him over to the body, seemingly of their own free will. Jake knelt beside the corpse and lifted its head with the barrel of his gun.

"Doc?"

"It's Mr. Skinner our janitor."

Jake closed his eyes with a mixture of sadness and relief.

"What do we do now?" asked Mary.

"We continue with the plan," Jake replied.

"What about those footprints heading back up the stairs?" Shams asked.

"There's two sets of prints. Looks like someone was gettin' chased. Jake's right though. We need to check this place out room by room. We don't need no surprises," answered Bill.

"Are you just going to leave him here?"

Jake rounded on Mary, "Yes that's exactly what WE'RE going to do. Once we've made sure we're the only ones here we'll come back for him."

They filed out onto the lowest floor, not looking at one another.

Bill moved alongside Jake and asked him quietly, "Are you okay?"

"Yeah, I'm fine...peachy."

"Any volunteers for stairwell duty?" he asked a little too loudly and more than a little coldly, startling everyone.

They knew the body in the stairwell had upset Jake but nobody knew what to say. After all, they were counting on him.

After a few moments of awkward silence, Mary spoke.

"I'll go."

"Me too, I'll do it," Shams offered. "I'll go with Mary."

Everyone turned to look at Jameson who was trying not to be noticed.

"Jesus - yeah, why not?" he finally said.

"I'm proud of you Jameson. That a way to step up big boy," Bill said while grinning.

Jameson sneered and silently mouthed curses after Bill turned around.

"Jameson would you mind if Shams and I took the stairwell… without…without…"

"The dead guy?"

"Um, yeah. I wouldn't have been so callous about it though."

"Whatever," Jameson said after he turned away from Mary and began walking back toward the stairwell.

"What an ass," Mary whispered to herself.

"Great, I'll call out before and after each floor is cleared. We move up together. If you see or hear *anything* you shout out, understand? We do this as a team."

Bill and Jake watched as the rest of the group went to their appointed stairwells. Thunder boomed and shook the building once again.

"Are we a team?"

"What?"

"I asked you, are we a team? Are we together on this, because you're sure not acting like somebody that's got his head in the game."

Jake just stood there looking surprised.

"I know you're upset. Hell everybody knows somthin's botherin' ya, the way you been snappin' at everyone. Just don't take it out on 'em. There ain't no need in it."

"Are you finished?"

Bill stared at him with his shiny black eyes for what must've seemed to Jake like hours.

"I reckon I am."

"Good, you ready to do this?"

"Born ready."

Jake was thankful that Bill let it go. He was not somebody Jake wanted to tangle with.

"Which side of the hall do you want to search?" Jake asked.

"Always go right and you won't go wrong."

"Fair enough."

Pushing aside their emotions, the two men began searching each room on the floor. After an uneventful expedition, they finally reached the lab. The door was locked and appeared very battered, as if someone had tried to break down the door. Jake mopped his brow with a grimy shirtsleeve and breathed heavily as he stared at the door. Bill was watching Jake closely.

"Last time I was here I told Jennifer it would be safe. I told her to stay put. She was scared… didn't want me to leave. I let her down Bill."

"Look Doc, let's keep it together.. Just focus on what we're doin' here. I don't wanna be fightin' these things alone."

Jake looked at Bill without saying anything.

"Let's get this over with," Bill said.

Jake fished around in his pocket until his hand re-emerged with a set of keys covered in putrid goop.

"Don't shoot anything unless you're sure…sure that it's not…human."

Bill gave a quick nod and then focused intensely on the battered wooden entrance to the lab. Jake unlocked the door and tried to push it open but something was blocking it.

"What's wrong?"

"I don't know. Something's wedged against the door. I can't open it. Bill I'm going to try something. Jennifer! It's Dr. Northrop! Jennifer! I've got some help here with me! Are you in there? Open the door!"

"What the hell are you doing Doc? You want them things knowin' we're here?" hissed Bill.

Jake glanced over at Bill and said with a little grin, "You sound like Shams. Listen, now is good as any time. Besides, that door was barricaded from the inside. She might be alright!"

"Leave me alone. Go away. Just go away!" A voice whimpered from behind the door followed by weak crying. The sudden sound of another human being startled both men.

"Jennifer please, I've brought some people here that can help. Are you in there alone?" Nothing but soft crying met Jake's inquiry. "Are you okay? Where's Ruben?"

Her sobbing increased into a gut-wrenching wail followed by more soft, mournful crying.

"Jennifer I'm sorry I left you alone. Look I don't know what happened here but I need to get back into my lab. One of the people I brought with me is injured and we could really use your help."

"How do I know you're not like him?" Jennifer continued crying.

"Like who Jennifer? Jennifer, it's me Dr. Northrop. Nobody's going to hurt you okay?"

"No. Go away."

"Jennifer please, a man here is dying. He has a family. It doesn't have to be this way. I can help him but I need to get into my lab."

"GO AWAY!" Jennifer screamed as loudly as she could.

"Jennifer I know you're scared. But I'm not going to let a man die because you won't open this door. I didn't want to do it this way but if you don't open this door I'm going to blow it off its hinges. Just stand way back. I don't want you to get hurt from flying debris. Oh, and cover your ears."

"We ain't got nothing that can do that," Bill whispered.

"I know."

Bill understood and then nodded.

"Wait, don't! I'll open it. Just stand where I can see you."

There was a sound of someone dragging things across the floor followed by a few loud bangs as if heavy boxes were being dropped from a considerable height.

"You can come in but only you."

Jake laid down his gun and whispered to Bill, "I don't want to scare her."

Bill shook his head before whispering back, "I wouldn't do that if I were you."

Jake thought for a moment and decided to proceed.

"Okay, I'm coming in."

He pushed at the door with a great deal of force causing it to open far enough for faint fluorescent light from a toppled-over desk lamp to spill out into the hall. Jake was barely able to see inside the lab. There were boxes and papers scattered all over the floor and several folders were still wedged underneath the door.

"That's far enough! I want to see your face! I need to know it's really you!"

"Fine, I'm going to step inside okay?"

"Yeah."

Jake slowly forced half his body inside the door through the narrow opening while having to step over file folders. He peered into the darkened lab to see a figure preparing to hack at him with something.

"Stop it's me Dr. Northrop!"

A light shone directly in his face blinded him suddenly so he raised his hands to protect his eyes. Thunder crashed again causing Jake to jump.

"Lower your hands!"

"It's me Dr…"

"DO IT NOW!"

"Okay just don't hit me with… whatever that is," Jake blinked as the light remained in his face.

"Dr. Northrop?"

"Will you please get that light out of my face now?"

Jennifer ran to Jake and hugged him tightly. "Oh thank God it's you. Oh yuck you smell horrible!" she said while pushing him away.

"Jennifer, where's Ruben?"

She started crying and held him again. He felt sticky wetness sinking into his shirt and pulled away from her.

"You're hurt. Who did this to you Jennifer?" He held her arm in his hand and gently rolled it over. He could see that she was injured but couldn't ascertain the severity of her wounds in the poor lighting. She shook her head back and forth all the while still clinging to Jake.

"Everything alright in there?"

"Come on in Bill and turn the lights on. Jennifer, I want you to meet someone. This is…"

Abruptly she pushed Jake away and began backing up.

"No, this isn't right. I'm sorry. I'm so, so sorry. You have to leave now - IT'S A TRAP!"

"What?"

Jake struggled to see in the dim light but couldn't make out anything past Jennifer. Enveloped by sudden pain, Jake's mind seemed to explode with bright, bluish-white light as he was slammed facedown into the floor. Off in the distance he could hear thunder and someone screaming faintly. He wondered to himself who it could be. If only he could think but his head was hurting so badly. Maybe they needed help. Maybe he was only imagining it or he was dreaming. Then sounds rang out from every direction-strange muffled pops or fireworks.

*Yes, fireworks, that's what they are. Wait, no this isn't right.* Jake thought. Everything was spinning. He knew he was going to be sick. He realized someone was dragging him across a floor but didn't know who it was or why they were doing it. He tried putting his hands out to stop himself but didn't have the strength. A foul odor enveloped him causing waves of nausea. It proved too much and he began to vomit. Just then he felt himself flying through the air only to be overwhelmed with pain again as he crashed into something immovable. As he lay slumped against the back wall, he awoke from his stupor long enough to see muzzle flashes erupting from somewhere nearby. His body shook so hard he wouldn't be able to stand if he wanted too and right now he just wanted to lay here. Someone was standing over him though he couldn't tell who. He reached out his hand instinctively only to have it twisted around so painfully that he momentarily forgot about the pain in his head.

As he cried out in agony, a terrible, wet, and raspy voice growled into Jake's face.

"You like that huh? Oh I've waited so long for this! You're pathetic! You're all pathetic!" The horrible stench that came with that voice nearly sent him back into unconsciousness. Jake couldn't remember who he was or why someone was trying to kill him but he knew it was so.

"Stop please! What do you want? I'll do whatever you want!" Jake wailed.

Bill ran his only hand along the inside wall beside the door, desperately trying to find the light switch. He couldn't risk not being able to see the enemy so he gave up his fruitless search and aimed his weapon's flashlight at Jake's attacker.

"Doc stay down! I can't get a clear shot!"

His attacker hoisted Jake to his feet; pinning his arms painfully behind his own back. All he could see was a bright light shining from a distant part of the room. He turned his face away from that piercing light and his cheek met with rotting flesh.

"Go ahead brave little soldier. Shoot! Let's see if your aim is any good…Stumpy! Ha-ha! Ha-ha-ha-ha!" the horrible voice taunted.

Jake's senses began to return; that awful stench was bringing him back to the present. Something in that vengeful voice was familiar too. His current situation was now making sense, if only a little.

"Why are you doing this?" Jake asked.

"Stop! Don't hurt him, he can help you!"

Jake recognized this voice, *Jennifer? Jennifer!*

"He can't help anyone!"

"Ruben please!" She pleaded.

"I don't need help! You're the ones that need help!"

"Ruben? What, I don't understand. What's happened to you?" Jake asked. And then Jake's cell phone began to ring.

Ruben tightened his hold on Jake's arms, stretching his shoulder tendons beyond their limits. He grimaced in pain but could do nothing to stop it.

"Don't play stupid with me professor! Do you take me for a fool?" Ruben plucked the phone out of Jake's pocket with one hand while maintaining an iron grip on Jake's wrists with the other hand. A sardonic smile twisted his rotting face as he answered Jake's phone.

"What?"

"I heard gunfire. Is everything okay?" Chris asked nervously.

"Yeah, where are you?"

Bill and Jennifer began yelling over one another, "No don't listen to him! It's not Jake!" Bill screamed.

"Help! Help us! Send help please!" Jennifer screamed at the same time, drowning out Bill's warning.

"Who was that? What's going on? Are you sure everything's okay? Look I'm where you left us, on the first floor with Carl. I haven't moved. Carl's still unconscious. Hello? Hello Jake? Shit the line's dead."

Ruben chuckled, a deep, evil laugh as he dropped the phone on the floor. His grotesque smile transformed into a snarl as he pulled Jake back up to his mouth.

"I'm going to enjoy this. Look at me! LOOK AT ME! You did this! You're going to suffer like me! Now you'll know real pain!"

With one thunderous bang, the standoff was over. The air exploded from the professor's lungs. Jake's legs betrayed him and folded beneath his body like an empty paper sack. He was simply a marionette whose strings had been severed. Jennifer watched in disbelief as he crumpled in slow motion. During those precious few seconds between life and death, Jake Northrop was filled with longing and regret. And in his final moment of consciousness, that awful, hate-filled voice raged like fire and consumed his soul.

# CHANGES

**November 28th:**

Bill stood in the doorway, his gun held at the ready, black eyes unblinking. With inhuman speed, Ruben lunged. At the last possible moment, Bill shifted his left shoulder allowing Ruben to crash past him into the hallway wall. Bill simply shut the door behind him and locked it. Immediately gunfire erupted in the hallway along with a roar that could only be the creature howling in frustration. Ignoring the fighting, Bill quickly moved toward the still form of Jake. He laid his weapon down and knelt beside the professor.

"Doc? Come on buddy…say something."

"You shot him! Look what you did! You killed him you idiot!" shouted Jennifer.

"Turn on some lights girl! I need to see what I'm doin!"

Jennifer ran to the wall and with a click, the white room was awash with light.

With a great deal of effort, the now wild-eyed Bill ripped open Jake's shirt and stared at the center of his chest - where the bullet had hit its mark. He sat back on his haunches and let out a long breath. Bill buried his grimy head in his hand and then, while shaking his head softly said, "Son of a bitch."

Jake croaked, "You shot me," as he clutched his chest and attempted to sit up.

"Professor, you're not dead!" shouted Jennifer while running toward Jake.

"Give 'im some room girl." Bill shooed her away and focused his attention on Jake.

"I thought I'd killed you…scared me half to death," Bill complained as he helped Jake right himself.

Jake ran his hand underneath the thin body armor and examined his chest.

"Oh God, I still might die. Christ I think my sternum is broken. How did you know I was wearing the vest?" Jake groaned.

"I didn't. I was trying to shoot that asshole in the head."

Jake looked up at Bill with a mixture of surprise and disbelief.

Bill started laughing at the expression on Jake's face, "I'm just messin' with you. I figured you'd put it on."

"And shooting me was the best plan you could come up with?" inquired Jake incredulously.

"I couldn't risk hittin' you somewhere that didn't have armor."

"Why didn't you just use the E.M.P.?"

"Well at first I didn't know he was one of them things. By the time I figured it out it wouldn't charge. I guess the flashlight was drainin' the battery this whole time."

"And shooting me was the only option?"

"That thing was hell bent on kickin' your ass Doc. I figured if I took away his play toy it'd piss 'im off enough to get careless."

"You shot me!"

"If you hadn't of followed my advice you'd be dead right now. I told you that armor would come in handy."

"Did you kill him?" Jake groaned while still holding his chest.

"No but it sounded like he…"

"Hey you guys ok? Unlock the door!" Mary shouted. "I think we killed it! Hey let us in!"

As Bill went to open the door, Jake warned him, "Careful, it may be a..."

"Trap?" Bill was looking directly at Jennifer when he completed Jake's sentence.

Jake nodded. Jennifer folded her arms across her chest, stamped her foot, and rolled her eyes toward the ceiling and away from Bill's gaze. Bill made a small grunting noise and turned back toward the door with a look of disgust on his face. Bill looked back at Jake who was grimacing but holding the rifle steady. He yanked open the door and met the barrel of Mary's gun.

"Easy now, we wouldn't want someone gettin' hurt."

"Bill, thank God! Is everybody ok? We heard gunshots and all this screaming. We came to see what was going on and saw that thing charging through the door. We shot it. It's ok now."

Bill poked his head outside the lab to view Ruben's corpse, "Where'd it go?"

"What do you mean where'd it go?"

Mary began speaking as she and Shams turned back toward the hallway, "It's right…it was right there just a second ago!"

Chris was standing next to Carl with his gun aimed at the door. Nervous beads of sweat rolled down his jaw as he stared at the gloomy wooden door. Thankfully the storm outside was subsiding. He'd never liked storms, they always made him nervous. But now his mind was wandering and he couldn't seem to concentrate. He kept thinking it would be great to get out of his filthy clothes and take a shower. Nothing had gone right for him. He'd lost everything in the space of a day and now it seemed he was losing his mind. He began to chuckle nervously at that last thought and wiped at his forehead with the back of his hand. He knew something had happened downstairs. There'd been gunfire and screaming. It could only mean the others had run into more of the walking dead. Jake had told him everything was ok, so Chris waited with superhuman patience. Even for someone with veins full of adrenaline it had been a very long day and he was exhausted. When the lights went out unexpectedly, it served only to further darken his mood.

"Crap, that figures."

The rifle strap was cutting into his shoulder so he decided it would be a good time to attempt another call to Jake. He leaned his back against the wall, bent his knees and allowed his upper body to slide down until his bottom touched the floor. Unseen to any eye, a brownish-streak of filth marked his descent. Now he could prop the rifle on his knees while using the phone.

"Come on, answer."

"Chris is that you?" answered Jake finally.

"Yeah, you guys alright down there?"

"Chris, stay put we're coming to get you okay. I don't have time to explain just sit tight."

"Why what's going on? I really don't want to stay here anymore. I'd feel a lot better if I were with you guys. Wait, I hear someone coming. Jake is that you? Man you got here fast."

"Chris, wait! No, don't let him in. Chris? Chris!"

Relieved and excited by the prospect of being with a group of people again, Chris closed the phone and tucked it into his pocket before he could hear Jake's warning.

Without looking at Carl or expecting a reply from him, he picked himself up off the floor and said, "Alright, looks like we're on the move again."

Feeling rejuvenated, he slung the rifle over his shoulder and hurried toward the door.

"Man I'm glad to see you...," he said as he opened it.

Confusion set in as Chris stared into the blackness of the hallway.

"Jake?"

He cautiously poked his head out of the door while holding onto the frame with both hands. He looked to the left and then to the right but could see nothing.

"Hmmmm...somebody there?"

There was no answer. He turned his back to the darkened hallway, again using the doorjamb to steady himself as he spoke to Carl.

"Nobody's there."

A sound resembling a mixture of someone biting into a crisp green apple and a hungry dog eating raw-liver occurred a split second before Chris began to scream. A pair of cold hands grabbed both sides of his head and quickly wrenched it around, immediately silencing his cry. When Ruben released his head, Chris's lifeless corpse dropped to its knees and fell forward, coming to rest chest down on the floor inside the classroom. He resembled a life-sized Ken doll whose head had been carelessly twisted around to face the wrong direction by some playful child. For a moment, dead eyes met one another as Chris stared helplessly up at Ruben. With hands still outstretched, Ruben tilted his head to the side and gazed at the messy jets of blood still spurting out across the floor from Chris's wrist. Ruben raised his eyebrows and, even though he no longer needed to, he blinked very slowly and sighed as if he were somehow remorseful. Ruben turned to look at Blaine who stood there beside him with a huge gob of flesh and bone hanging out of his mouth.

"You're still an idiot," Ruben said while shaking his head and stepping over Chris's body.

He then saw Carl slumped against the wall inside the classroom. Ruben jogged over and knelt beside him. He didn't have much time before the others showed up. Ruben hesitated for a moment before deciding to take him along. He easily lifted Carl's limp body and slung him over his shoulder. As he exited the classroom, he heard people coming up the stairs but that didn't concern him anymore. There were more important things to do now that he had a purpose again. Uninterested in Ruben or Carl, Blaine began shuffling away. Wads of meat slipped carelessly from his mouth as he lumbered down the hall with no destination whatsoever.

Jake was the first to come out of the stairwell and he saw someone or something moving down the hall leaving behind a trail of blood and meat.

"Hey you! Hold it right there! Who are you? Ruben?"

Jake looked around at the classrooms on either side to make sure he wasn't stumbling into another trap. His flashlight had grown dim but he could see that there was someone lying on the classroom floor where Chris and Carl were supposed to be.

"Shit."

"Damn it Doc wait up!" shouted Bill, who was just now entering the hallway where Jake stood motionless.

Once again the professor focused his attention on the dark hallway before him. The shuffling noise was gone along with the dim likeness of a human being. A low, throaty moan echoed in the darkened hallway sending chills up the two men's spines. The shuffling noise resumed as the thing began moving once more. Bill shined his flashlight on the creature and Jake immediately recognized Blaine.

"Blaine? Oh God."

"God ain't got nothin' to do with that Doc."

Jake's ears burned from the implications of Bill's statement. Bill aimed his rifle at Blaine but Jake stopped him from firing.

"Hang on a second!"

"Doc that thing ain't your student no more!"

"I know, I know, just wait a second! I want to try something. Blaine can you understand me? It's Dr. Northrop. I don't want to hurt you. I want to help you."

"Come on Doc what are you doin'? You know that thing can't understand you. Look at him!"

"Maybe so but you saw what Rube…that other one could do." Jake refused to call the creature that had attacked him by name only to dehumanize it and lessen the pain and guilt he felt.

Blaine continued his slow shuffle toward the pair without acknowledging anything Jake had said.

"Blaine, do you remember me?"

Shams and Mary were now standing beside Bill; both had their rifles aimed at Blaine. Jennifer held her face in her hands and refused to look up. As Blaine approached Jake, it was apparent that there was nothing intelligent beyond his blank stare. Even so, Jake wanted to study this creature and find out what made it tick. Deep down inside what he really wanted was to capture and study Ruben. Why was he so different from Blaine and why did Ruben want so desperately to kill him? His thoughts were interrupted by a gunshot and the gruesome visual of Blaine's head exploding.

*"What are you doing?"* Jake screamed.

"What you couldn't do," Mary answered.

"YOU IDIOT! I wanted to figure out what happened, not read him bedtime stories!"

"That's the problem! You called IT a HIM! You think that thing is still a person? That person is DEAD! Do you understand? That thing is not a person and IT doesn't have a name!" Mary screamed back at Jake.

"I know that these things come in at least two flavors," Jake said holding up two fingers for emphasis.

"Like that one there that you just shot, and like the one downstairs that attacked me. You weren't there but let me tell you something. That one…he knew who I was, he knew how to talk, and he was pissed off! He wasn't the person he used to be but he had that person's memories and God damn it I want to know why! The only way I can do that is to get one of these things and study it BEFORE it's destroyed."

"Doc's right. I saw that one downstairs and thought it was alive. It acted just like a man."

"Guys come here! You need to see this! It's Chris!" Shams shouted excitedly.

Everyone crowded around the doorway staring at Chris's broken body with no one saying a word.

"Where's Carl?" Jake asked suddenly as he pushed past everyone and stepped into the classroom.

He grabbed Mary's rifle and scanned the room with the attached flashlight that was much brighter than his own. There were bloody footprints leading to the wall where Carl had lain.

"Where is he?" asked Shams, as he craned his neck around Bill and struggled to see into the room.

"He ain't here that's for sure," said Bill.

Jennifer stood just inside the doorway, clutching Bill's denim jacket and shaking her head as she looked back down at Chris.

"Well I don't think he walked out of here by himself," Jake stated as he shone light on the footprints.

"Doc are you thinkin'…"

"Yeah, Ruben took him," Jake interrupted.

"Why? What would it want with Carl?" asked Mary as she and Shams finally gathered the nerve to step over the corpse and into the darkened classroom.

Jake paused for a moment as if contemplating something.

"I don't know. Here, take your rifle back."

"That's it! From now on we maintain visual contact with one another at all times!" Shams commanded in his thick Bengali accent, surprising everyone.

"Wait a minute, where's Jameson?" inquired Jake.

"I don't know. We haven't seen him. I guess he's still in the other stairwell," said Mary as she looked back and forth between Shams and Jake.

Suddenly Jennifer screamed.

"Doc!"

Everybody turned and saw the reason for Jenifer and Bill's excitement. Chris' head was slowly moving from side to side. His mouth began to open and close while his eyes were rolling around in their sockets. It was a ghastly sight that reminded Jake of the lab rabbit that refused to die.

"He was infected? How? Is this what's gonna to happen to us?" Mary asked.

"He was bitten," Jake replied.

"Was anybody else here bitten?" Shams asked.

Mary put her head into her hands and began to cry.

"Were you bitten?" Shams asked Mary while he began backing away from her.

"Now isn't the time for this. Help me get him down to my lab. I need to find out how to stop this."

"When is a better time for you? When she turns into a zombie and tries to kill you…or me?" Shams asked Jake in an accusatory tone.

"It's not like that. I didn't say anything before because I wasn't sure. I'm still not sure. At first, I thought it took…weeks, a month maybe. Some people get sick and die soon after they're infected. Others seem to get sick and then they feel fine…no symptoms. Chris and his wife were bitten several days ago. She got sick and just kept getting worse until she died. She became one of those things but could barely move. Chris said he felt bad for a while but then he got better. I think it depends on how long someone is infected. The longer you've been infected then the more likely you are to end up as one of those things."

"This is supposed to make me feel better?" Mary sobbed.

"What I'm trying to say is that time's on our side. This is an infection. Infections can be stopped but we have to work fast. I need answers. And just so you all know, before we get paranoid and turn on one another, being bitten is probably not the only way to get infected. For all I know… we're all infected. Just give me a hand here."

"What about Jameson?" Shams asked.

"We can look for him later. If he hasn't come out of his hiding place before now he probably won't, so he's safe. But first let's go take a look at that front door and see if our friend left us anything to lock."

They walked hastily to the front of the darkened building and found that the front door was indeed unlocked.

"Well he does have keys to the building," Jake stated.

"At least he didn't break the glass," Mary added.

"What if he comes back?" Shams asked.

"I don't know. We can try and wedge the door closed but look…"

Jake waved his hands at the front of the building.

"It's all glass. Let's just get Chris downstairs and do what we came here to do, as fast as we can do it," he concluded.

Seeing that there was nothing else to be done about the building's security, they set about the uneasy task of getting their deceased comrade's body down to the professor's lab.

"Hey Doc, can't we just cut the head off and take that downstairs? I'm afraid someone's gonna get bit tryin' to carry the whole thing down."

"No, I want to see how the infection spread through his body and to do that I need all of him in one piece. Let's just pull his shirt over his head and we can tie it in place. It may not stop him from biting but at least we won't have to look at him."

Jake and Bill pulled Chris' filthy shirt over his head and wrapped it tightly around his neck. They then tied it off in the front leaving a large knot of cloth over his mouth.

"Now we'll just drag him down the stairs by his legs. You and Shams grab that side and I'll get this side."

With a great deal of effort that included liberal amounts of swearing, they dragged Chris' body down the stairs and into the lab. A streak of blood and filth marked their passage.

"Now we need to get those lights back on. We should stick together. We'll look for Jameson on our way to the electrical panel, agreed?"

"Yeah," replied Bill as the rest of the group nodded in agreement.

Jennifer walked beside Jake so she could talk to him without the others hearing.

"Professor, Ruben told me that he did something…stole some of the bacteria we used to inject the rabbits. He said he was going to buy us…me and him… a new future."

"What did he do with it?"

"I'm not sure…"

"Think Jennifer. I need to know."

"Sell it I guess."

"To who? Who was he going to sell it to?"

"I don't know. He said that they were going to pay him enough that we would never have to worry about money again. That's why he was so mad at you. He thinks you took that away from him."

"I was so blind…I had no idea he was stealing from me. I trusted him."

"Professor, something else…what you said back there about being bitten…Ruben…well he bit me."

"Damn, I'm sorry. I knew you were hurt but I didn't know…"

"That's not all." Jennifer interrupted.

"In some ways he was still, you know, Ruben but…he was twisted and…what he did to me was…" Jennifer trailed off and looked as though she were drifting off to sleep.

"What did he do Jennifer? It's okay, you can tell me."

Her demeanor changed abruptly from visibly distraught to seductive as the infection took over her mind.

"Never mind it's nothing. Let's talk about you and me," she said through parted lips that she slowly licked.

"What?" Jake spluttered while blinking his eyes quickly and shaking his head.

"I've seen the way you look at me professor. I know you want me," Jennifer said in a bedroom-voice full of lust.

"What the hell has gotten into you?" he whispered loudly.

Jake became aware that the others had stopped walking and were staring at the two of them. "I'm sorry but I…this is…this is not you talking," he whispered in a stern, fatherly voice.

"You guys okay?" asked Shams.

Jake looked at Jennifer and nodded.

"Look it's…it's...we can talk about this later. We need to get the power on okay?"

Jennifer looked very confused as if she had been prematurely awakened from a dream.

"Jennifer, are you listening to me? You don't look so well."

Jennifer nodded but said nothing. Jake looked at her worriedly for a moment before turning towards Bill.

"Doc where's the breaker panel?"

"The elevator room, it's this way — to the left. Down here," Jake said while walking on ahead and pointing down the hall. His heavily falling feet echoed like the steady rhythm of textile machinery in some distant mill, *clip-clop, clip-clop, clip-clop*. He stopped abruptly in front of two wooden doors that consumed the light that fell upon them. They were positioned adjacent to a stairwell, the same stairwell Jameson was supposed to guard. Jake's dying flashlight wandered over a sign above the doors. In white lettering engraved on a black plastic panel was written, *Authorized Personnel Only.*

*Twin guardians of the abyss,* Jake thought to himself while looking at the doors. His thoughts then circled around and landed on something he'd read a long time ago. He remembered the inscription at the entrance to Hell in Dante's Divine Comedy, "All hope abandon ye who enter here".

*I'm already in Hell, how can it get any worse?* he asked himself.

"Okay, everybody ready?" asked Jake when suddenly there was a banging sound from within the room.

"What was that?" Shams asked.

"Hmmm… the door isn't locked so we're about to find out," Jake said while twisting the door handle downward.

He tugged the door open and instantly everyone shined their feeble lights into the darkness.

"Don't shoot! Don't shoot! It's me!" screamed a panic-stricken Jameson.

"What the hell are you doing in here? Where were you earlier? Didn't you hear all the fighting?" asked Jake.

"I was guarding the stairwell like you said."

"Oh horse shit!" Jake retorted.

"No listen, when I heard the gunfire I came out into the hall to see what was going on and that's when I heard someone in the stair well above me. I walked up to the next flight of stairs and saw someone or... something so I started following it. When I heard more shooting, I ran back down here. That's when I saw someone go into this room and I thought it was one of you. I walked in here and that's the last thing I remember. Next thing I know you're all pointing guns at me!"

"I think you're a bad liar *and* a coward," Shams snapped at Jameson.

"I swear to God!" replied Jameson.

"Doc he could be tellin' the truth. His head's bleedin'."

"Yeah and it feels like it's gonna explode," whined Jameson.

"Enough! Let's get the lights turned on," commanded Jake.

"I swear I'm telling the truth!" Jameson whispered excitedly to Shams.

"SHUT UP! Open your mouth one more time and *I'll* split your skull!" shouted Jake.

"Geez okay already, you don't have to..." Jameson was saying just before Jake lunged at him.

Bill and Shams grabbed the professor and held him back.

"Easy Doc! Come on now. You don't want to do this!"

"Keep him away from me! He's crazy!" Jameson shrieked.

This only fueled Jake's rage and he fought that much harder to free himself. Jameson backed up a couple of steps and then collapsed on the floor. Jake stopped struggling and stood there breathing heavily.

"What's wrong with him?" asked Mary.

"It looked like he got hit on the head," replied Bill.

"Maybe he just fainted," Shams chimed in.

"Let's bring him to my lab. But let me find that circuit breaker first. My flashlight's dead; shine yours over here."

Shams pointed his rifle at Jake and then at the panel beside him. Jake opened it and found that the main breaker had been tripped. With a sharp snap, he flipped it back into the normal position and washed away the darkness.

"Alright, grab an arm, grab a leg," Jake commanded.

They lifted Jameson and began carrying him down the hall. After a few steps, he regained consciousness and began to flail about.

"Put me down! Put me down! Where are you taking me?"

"Let him down," Jake sighed to Shams.

"You fainted so we were taking you back to the lab," explained Jake.

"You get away from me you psychopath!"

"Fine," Jake said as he began walking back toward the lab.

The others watched Jake for a moment before looking back at Jameson and then again at Jake's back. One at a time, they decided to follow the professor. Jameson was being left behind…again.

"Oh that's just great. Yeah, follow him. He's gonna get you all killed!" Jameson shouted.

He stood there watching everybody get farther and farther down the hall before he could no longer stand it.

"Hey wait! Don't leave me out here alone! Guys! Wait up!" Jameson pleaded as he jogged after the departing group.

Jake, Bill, and Shams dragged Chris' body through the lab until they ran into cages and equipment overturned in the earlier struggle between Jake and Ruben.

"I need to get him back to the dissection room. We have to move some of this stuff," Jake stated while looking up at Jameson.

Before Jameson could mouth a reply, Jennifer rolled her eyes toward the ceiling and began tossing overturned cages and boxes out of the way. Mary quickly pitched in. Jameson moved toward the two as if to offer help but grimaced and held his head in his hands; nobody paid him any attention. Once they finally got the corpse into the dissection room, it proved an even greater task getting it up on the stainless steel table.

"Fudge monkey, he's heavy!" Jake groaned as they hoisted the corpse into the air.

"What'd you say Doc?"

"Nothing---I was---trying---to be---funny," Jake blurted between each renewed attempt to overcome gravity.

"You're a---very strange man--- Jake," Shams grunted as they unsuccessfully attempted to raise Chris' body up to the table.

"Wait, wait. Put him down," Jake grunted like a disappointed power lifter.

"This isn't going to work," he announced.

"Damn he's heavy," Shams said incredulously.

"We need someone supporting his mid-section. Mary, Jennifer can you two pick him up in the middle while we hoist him up from the ends?" Jake asked between deep exhalations of air.

With the extra muscle, they unceremoniously plopped Chris' body onto the dissection table. Jake immediately started assembling the items he would need to conduct the autopsy. He positioned Chris' head so that he could easily reach the base of his skull. Everyone else hovered around the outer edges of the room occasionally shooting uneasy glances toward the far end of the outer lab and the locked door.

At last the professor was ready. He removed the knotted shirt from around Chris' head and stared at the creature's shifting and contorting face. Jake leaned down for a closer look and the seemingly random movement of the creature's eyes ceased when they locked onto him. Its angry red eyes, dry from death and beginning to cloud over, followed Jake's every move. The thing was no longer a pathetic likeness of a human. It was a big cat stalking its prey. Its lips curled back over gleaming white teeth and dead, grayish-blue gums. Jake strapped its head to the table and threaded another strap through its mouth, effectively preventing it from closing any further. He reached up and turned on the fume hood and the fan came loudly to life. Now the autopsy could begin.

Jake started at the back of Chris' head, incising his scalp from ear to ear. Dark rivulets of congealing blood oozed slowly down to the table and then refused to move any further. Mary and Jennifer couldn't watch any longer and turned their backs to the horrible scene.

"Shouldn't you kill it or put it out of its misery first?" Jennifer said squeamishly.

Jake ignored the comment and continued working. The others stood transfixed as he worked his gloved fingers beneath the large flap of flesh and hair at the back of Chris' head. With one smooth motion, he peeled Chris' scalp over his skull like a rubber Halloween mask. Using a bone-saw, the professor removed the entire top half of the skull revealing a dark, stringy, and resinous looking substance that nearly prevented him from pulling the two halves apart.

"What the hell's that?" Bill asked Jake while stroking his grimy beard and grimacing.

"I've seen it before. One of those things that attacked me…had this stuff holding it all together. I think I know what it is. It's spider silk."

"It's what?" asked Bill.

"I engineered the bacteria to produce it. It was meant to hold the neural networks together while I…removed them from the rabbits."

"Nice job," Jameson said while smiling.

Jake glared at Jameson for a moment before asking Bill to turn out the lights.

"Doc what's that you're holdin'?"

"This? It's a hand-held Ultraviolet light. My bacteria fluoresce green so I should be able to see how far they've spread with a simple glance," he explained while pointing to the device in his hand.

"You mean a Black Light?" Bill asked

"Well, yes."

"Why didn't you just say that?" Bill asked as he reached for the light switch.

Jake considered a stinging reply to Bill's question as he stared at the blurry purple glow emanating from the light in his hand but dismissed the idea when his eyes caught the ghostly green glow of the bacteria. He bent down over the open skull and pointed at it.

"Yeah, it's my bacteria alright. Look here. You see this? See how brightly this is glowing? Look at how it's invaded all this tissue. Man, and after only four or five days too. That just can't be right. Still, I need to look at it under the microscope to be certain," he said while shaking his head and blinking quickly.

"You mean it shouldn't of spread that fast?"

Jake sighed heavily.

"This stuff shouldn't have even infected peo...ple..." as Jake turned his head to look at Bill he stopped talking and abruptly stood upright. His expression made it clear that something was wrong. Jake extended the light toward Bill and the others without saying a word.

"Doc what's a matter?"

Bill looked down and noticed his denim jacket and shoelaces were struggling to emit a pale bluish-glow through the grime on them. He followed Jake's gaze to his right and then he saw it. Everyone saw it, except for one.

"You guys, you're freaking me out okay! What are you staring at?" Jennifer asked nervously.

Jake spoke first.

"Have you been experiencing any strange moods or felt...different lately?"

"What? No! God what's wrong with you people? Is there something on me?" Jennifer shouted as she inspected her clothing and hands.

"Oh man I knew this was gonna happen! I freakin' knew it!" complained Jameson.

"Shut up! You're not helpin' here!" snapped Bill.

Jake attempted to calm her down.

"Just relax."

"You relax! You're all staring at me like a bunch of freaks! What's on me?"

Jennifer caught a glowing reflection in the mirror above the sink. She wasn't sure it was her until she moved closer to the mirror and raised her hands to her mouth. She didn't understand what she was seeing. Large, jagged circles of glowing green circumscribed her lips and eyes. Her mouth hung open in surprise, allowing her to see the glow inside. Fluorescent streaks traced the path of tears down her face.

“Professor, I don’t…I don’t understand. What is this? What’s happening to me?”

Except for Jake, everyone began backing away from Jennifer.

“I already told you, we’re probably all infected…to some degree.”

“Infected! You mean I have that stringy crap in my head!”

“Listen to me. This is why we’re here. I can help you if you let me.”

Jennifer’s eyes rolled toward the ceiling.

“No really, just give me a chance and I…Jennifer?”

Only the whites of her eyes were showing and she was beginning to foam at the mouth.

“Shit! Bill, get the lights!” Jake shouted.

Bill fumbled around on the wall but couldn’t seem to find the light switch. His hand was shaking uncontrollably. Jennifer gurgled something that sounded like the word no before she fell to the floor and began to spasm violently. The veins stood out from her arms, neck, and head like writhing serpents slithering just beneath turbid water.

“Turn the lights on! Turn ‘em on!” Jake shouted.

“I’m tryin’!”

“Get out of my way! Let me outta here!” screamed Jameson.

“Holy shit!” Shams exclaimed while pressing his back up against the wall farthest from the spectacle.

Jennifer’s back suddenly arched so tightly that only her head, feet, and the back of her wrists were in contact with the floor. She then fell over onto one side with her body remaining unnaturally bent. Without saying anything Jake rushed past Shams and Bill and disappeared into the lab.

“Move! I’m getting out of here too!” Shams yelled at Bill who was still struggling to find the light switch.

Bill was panicking. The tremors had started unexpectedly in his hand the moment he saw that Jennifer was in trouble. His heart was pumping furiously and his head was pounding. It had been far too long since he last had a drink. His alcohol-deprived body was betraying him. He was ashamed of himself and felt worthless again; the useless alcoholic was letting everyone down.

*Not this time damn it! Not now!* Bill silently screamed at himself.

He finally managed to turn the lights on just as Jake came back in with a syringe. Jake dropped down onto the floor beside Jennifer and administered the shot directly into her neck. He held her steady while the tranquilizer began to work. He reached into his pocket and removed another syringe.

"What are you doin' Doc?"

"Stopping her seizure but...her body's fighting the infection. The only problem with that is..." Jake stopped talking as he uncapped the syringe with his teeth, spit the cap out on the floor and pushed the plunger down just far enough for a little squirt of liquid to erupt from the tip of the needle.

"...that's exactly the thing that's going to kill her," Jake answered as he administered the second shot into her arm.

Jennifer's body began to relax and soon was no longer rigid.

"I don't understand. Don't you need to find somethin' that'll kill this stuff?" Bill said while trying to stop his hand from trembling by making a fist in his pocket.

"Yes...but in her case it seems that the infection has progressed too far."

"Then what are you goin' to do?"

"Try to keep her stable until I get some more answers. I just gave her an immune suppressant along with the tranquilizer. Maybe it'll help with the seizures...I don't know."

"Can't you give her some antibiotics?"

"Not if her disease is as far along as I think it is. I'm trying to slow her immune response right now. Some people with this infection...they may have symptoms similar to those caused by Lupus or other autoimmune disorders but only much worse. Others may not have any symptoms at all, they just up and die. It's that way for many diseases. I'm sure the reaction is different depending on the person. Come to think of it, most of the people in the E.R. had flu-like symptoms, but there were some psychotic patients too. Strange, those were more like end-stage rabies infections though. In Jennifer's case, I think it may be causing inflammation around her brain. It could be why she's having seizures."

"Or like she said doc, her head could be filled with that stringy crap."

"Maybe, but a host's reaction to a parasite is often worse than the infection itself."

"You can't tell me that havin' a head full of parasites isn't that bad."

"That's not what I'm saying. I know it's bad. I'm trying to lessen the damage her body is doing to itself while it fights the infection. Look I didn't engineer this stuff to kill. That's not what successful parasites do to their host."

"Yeah but we're not supposed to be its host are we? And look what happened when you put that crap in them rabbits."

Jake thought for a moment before answering.

"The bacteria didn't kill the rabbits."

"What? But you said…"

"It wasn't the direct cause."

Jake looked down at the ground and blinked hard, his forehead furrowed in thought. Resigned to Bill's reaction, he looked up at him before he said it.

"It formed a sort of symbiotic relationship with them."

"Symbiotic…what the fu…look around you man! How can you say that?" Bill said in a quavering voice.

"Maybe you hit the nail on the head Bill. When a parasite jumps species it usually becomes more deadly."

"So what?"

"It's not in a parasite's best interest to kill its host. That is, not until it can be transmitted to another organism. And it's like you said, we're not its primary host. This species of bacteria was engineered to live in rabbits not humans. That may be why it's lethal to us. It also seems to alter the behavior of its victims."

"What?"

"Maybe so it can transmit itself to another host. It must compel the infected to get close enough to others so it can be transmitted through a bite. Jennifer was acting weird before all this went down. It was like a switch got flipped while she was talking to me. I mean she just changed all of a sudden, like she was hypnotized. And Ruben…I know it changed his behavior. Whatever he's become now, I'll bet you his behavior was radically different before he died."

Bill shook his head in disbelief.

"Radically different behavior? People are dyin' here doc! And these folks can still infect you after they're dead no matter how weird they were before they kicked the bucket."

"That's a side effect of the neural network patterning process."

"Jesus doc! You call makin' zombies outta folks a side effect!"

"I'm not trying to trivialize the horror of the situation Bill. I'm just trying to figure out a way to stop it or at least slow it down. And talking all this through helps me think so cut me some slack."

Bill rolled his eyes and shook his head dismissively. This irritated Jake to no end. He tilted his head to the side just a little and squinted at him, imagining Bill panhandling for money on the corner. Spoiling for a fight, he decided to take this further, to antagonize him with a little gem that would certainly bring him to the brink of apoplexy.

"So yeah… it's just a side effect," Jake sneered with all the arrogance of a bratty, young socialite.

Bill gawked at Jake, suddenly hearing what he had said. He tried to regain his composure as he struggled with his thoughts.

Jake smiled to himself, *Checkmate.*

Bill was seething with anger, fear, and desperation.

"How's this helpin' huh? How? I followed you here 'cause I thought you could fix this… I don't get you. What are you doin' to help us? What's your plan? Inject everyone with that, 'let's just all get along with one another crap', and hope that zombie shit plays nice? Well it won't! It'll kill you, me, her, all of us!"

Bill attempted to stroke his beard but his hand shook so hard that he quickly stuffed it back into his pocket but not before Jake saw.

"Bill, are you alright?"

"I'm fine."

"No you're not," Jake said matter-of-factly.

"Have you felt any different lately?"

"Don't you start that with me! This aint got nothin' to do with that crap you made!"

"Well then what's wrong?" Jake asked callously, seeing that Bill had walked right into his trap.

Instead of answering, he stomped away and into another room of the lab leaving Jake alone with just a corpse and his unconscious student for company.

*Oh well, what's done is done.*

Jake looked down at Jennifer as he ran his fingers through her soft, golden hair.

"I hope I'm doing the right thing. I don't know. I guess your dad was right after all. I just hope Ron's safe somewhere. Jesus what am I saying? No one's safe." Jake shook his head and looked up at the fluorescent lights.

"I had no idea what I was messing around with here did I? Maybe Bill's right too. Look at what I've already done," he lamented.

He absentmindedly swatted away a mosquito that had landed on his face. Jake Northrop looked back down at the beautiful young woman he cradled in his lap. He ground his teeth together as he once again thought of Heather.

His face contorted hideously as a sea of emotion welled up within him and threatened to wash away his sanity. Anger radiated from him like heat off a sun-baked desert.

"I'm doing the right thing! People ignored reason and that's why this is happening. If Ron hadn't of…" Jake trailed off as hot tears burned his face.

Moments later Bill and Shams poked their heads back into the room where Jake still sat cradling his student in his arms. They were afraid that Jake had succumbed to the same infection threatening Jennifer.

"Is everything ok in here?" Shams asked timidly.

"Go find a blanket so I can keep her warm," Jake snapped through gritted teeth.

"Right, sure…ok."

Not wanting to feel the heat of Jake's gaze any longer, Shams turned quickly and began his search for a blanket.

Jake looked down at Jennifer and was stroking her hair again when he told Bill his plan.

"I'm going to make an oral suspension of the antibiotics we used to help control the bacteria in the rabbits. As a preventative measure, I want everyone to begin taking it immediately. I don't have time to test it but it should buy us some time."

"I thought you said she was too far gone to take…"

"Everyone here will begin taking the antibiotics EXCEPT for Jennifer," the professor stated plainly, as he stared coldly at Bill.

"Yeah, no problem. I'll go tell everyone your *plan*."

"Get someone to help you take Jennifer out of here. I need to finish up with Chris. There are still questions I need answers to. After that, I'll try to contact the CDC. They need to know what they're up against," Jake explained as he carefully laid Jennifer's head down and stood up.

"Why are you still standing here?"

Not knowing how to respond to Jake's mercurial character, Bill opened his mouth and then immediately closed it. He felt like a confused child. Bill hadn't expected treatment this harsh from the professor. Instead of protesting, he looked away, sighed, and then left the room.

# NO JOY

**November 29**
**Arizona:**

It was after midnight and the sheriff and his patrol car were missing. No one had seen him since the violent attacks against his deputy, Joy, and the gas station attendant, Charlotte. Arizona state troopers had searched the area and found nothing but his badge, his gun, a shell casing, and a small puddle of blood.

Joy had insisted on riding out to the gas station to help look for the sheriff but the paramedics would not allow it because she was still bleeding badly. Instead, she had to rely on updates from the police scanner in the ambulance as they drove her to the hospital; the same hospital where she'd taken the sheriff after he was bitten by that deranged man. It'd been just over two weeks since that late night domestic disturbance call at the 'No Tell Motel' and now everything had changed. Even the arrogant doctor who had threatened her and the sheriff with criminal charges of abuse had died at the hands of that very same deranged man. And now the sheriff had changed.

Joy sat silently in the back of the ambulance with the paramedic and thought about how events seemed to have come full circle in such a short period of time. Her mind reeled from the onslaught of her own paradise lost. She wondered if this is how that man's wife felt after he had attacked her that night. Her whole world must've been pulled out from under her like the proverbial rug. She struggled to remember the woman's name but couldn't. It really didn't matter she thought. Her mind kept playing the same scenes of this nightmare over and over; that man biting the sheriff at the motel, the woman screaming at them not to hurt her husband, the doctor accusing her and the sheriff of murder, the camping trip where her own world was turned upside down, and the look on Roy's face right before he shot her. Even after that, Joy hoped the sheriff was somewhere safe. She loved him and she'd thought that

Roy loved her too. It was almost too much to bear. Tears filled her eyes, partly from the physical pain that she felt but mostly because her heart was utterly broken. She leaned over, held onto the edge of the gurney, and let the blood that had once again pooled in her mouth run down into the little white bucket by her side. She stared at the bright-red blood spatters that seemed to glow against the white plastic and was soon lost in her memories.

Joy remembered that night when she alone had gone back to the hospital to investigate the murder of the doctor. He had bled to death from a bite wound to his neck. She had stood over his lifeless body. Bright-red blood was splattered all over the floor and his crisp white coat. Her mind reconstructed his last few moments as if she had actually been there to see him lying on the cool tile, slipping into unconsciousness as his life-blood spurted out onto the floor with each beat of his failing heart. She wondered if he'd thought about the sheriff's warnings before he died. Even now, she felt sorry for him.

The orderly that she interviewed didn't actually see it happen either but he did see the man that the sheriff had brought in earlier that night leaving the room where the doctor was murdered. He told her that he saw the killer crawl out into the hall leaving a trail of blood after he'd heard the doctor's screams. He said that the doctor was unconscious and bleeding profusely from the wound to his neck when he'd entered the room. But by the time he went to get help, the killer had already fled and the doctor was dead. The trail of blood stopped at the emergency room exit. She'd wondered for weeks where he could've gone and why nobody saw him leave the hospital. They never found any trace of him after that.

*Frank, yes that was his name but what was his wife's name?* She asked herself.

This question was really beginning to bother her but she didn't understand why. She told herself that it didn't matter. The ambulance hit a bump in the road and she was painfully jolted back into the present.

"Hey take it easy up there! I got a patient back here you moron!" Burt yelled as he pounded the ambulance wall with his fist.

"I told you to lean back Joy. You're gonna bite the rest of your tongue off if that idiot hits another bump in the road," Burt admonished.

Joy wasn't listening to him. If she could just find out what was causing all this she might be able to help the sheriff. Just then, a more frightening thought occurred to her. What if she became delusional like Frank or Roy? Would she hurt those she loved too? No, she would simply end it and prevent this misery from spreading any further than it already had. But why hadn't the sheriff done that? She concluded that he must be too far gone to stop it

Joy knew him. She knew he would never hurt anyone on purpose. This scared her more than anything that had happened. The implications were easy to grasp. Once the madness set in it would be too late for her to do anything about it. She would become hopelessly insane and unable to stop herself. She wouldn't even be aware that it was happening.

"Damn it! Sit back Joy! I need to keep pressure on this wound," Burt commanded.

Obstinately Joy refused and just continued staring daggers at him. Burt tried to focus on the wound to her arm but found it difficult not to stare at her large, perfectly shaped breasts, which he could see clearly through the sheer material of her bloody tank top.

Joy grabbed Burt's arm, startling him, and motioned for something to write with. He handed her his pen and notepad while shaking his head.

"You're the worst patient I've ever had. You know that?"

Joy handed him a hastily scribbled note.

"What's this?" he asked.

Joy grabbed the note from him and slapped it hard against his chest.

"Jesus, what the hell's gotten into you?"

Joy jabbed her finger at the note and grimaced.

"Woman," Burt growled and then looked down at the note.

"Wait a minute, a quarantine? Are you serious? Why? On whose authority?"

Joy pointed to her chest and then to his. Once again, Burt found it difficult to take his eyes off her large, erect nipples protruding from the thin material of the tank-top. Burt shook his head and forced himself to look downward.

"Good Lord, would you please cover yourself? You're gonna get hypothermia," he moaned.

Burt turned his head and handed her a thermal blanket before continuing his speech.

"Look I know you've been under a lot of pressure lately but..."

With a loud crack Joy slapped Burt across the face just as he turned back to look at her.

"What the hell's wrong with you?" Burt yelled while rubbing his rapidly reddening face.

Joy grabbed the notepad from him, scribbled something else, and again slapped it against his chest.

"All right, all right! Stop with the police brutality will ya?"

Burt began reading the note and then looked up at Joy.

"So you think this is what happened to the sheriff? Rabies?

Joy shook her head and pointed to the note. Burt looked back down and continued reading.

*...Man that bit Roy had disease like rabies...bitten by a fox...not rabid.*

"So it's something like rabies but not rabies. Well what is it then? Never mind, of course you don't know. But that means you could be infected too doesn't it?"

Joy nodded and pointed back to the note.

*Call CDC, tell what happened... confine me to hospital... dangerous... find Roy!!!*

Burt sat down heavily with a grave look on his face.

"What do we quarantine, the hospital, the town, what?"

Burt handed her the notepad again and waited for her to reply to his questions.

Joy handed the pad back to him much more gently this time and then rested against the side of the ambulance. He read the note and then re-read it several times as if he expected the message to change. Without looking up at Joy, he read it aloud one last time.

"Williams and Flagstaff? A hospital, sure but we can't quarantine whole towns for something we're not even sure about. Flagstaff... you know they won't even..."

Burt stopped talking when he saw that Joy had passed out. Worriedly, he checked her vitals. Satisfied that she was just exhausted, he considered the quarantine. After several minutes of deep thought, he made up his mind. There would be no quarantine. Sure, he'll tell them to isolate the deputy just to be on the safe side and the sheriff *if* he could be found. But there was no way he was going to risk his career by stirring up trouble with wild ideas about a contagious disease. As far as he knew, only the sheriff and that fellow that attacked him had been violent. There wasn't any need to invoke some mysterious contagion to explain those things. In his opinion, the sheriff was a time bomb. Clearly, he had an aggressive Type-A-personality and that other guy was probably just whacked out on drugs.

Burt contemplated how to tell Joy he wasn't going along with her idea. He rubbed his face where she'd slapped him earlier and winced at the thought. Not wanting to risk something worse than a red face, he decided not to tell her. He didn't want anyone finding out about what had transpired between them so he crumpled the notes Joy had written and put the paper into his pocket.

Suddenly the ambulance swerved and there was a loud crash that sent Burt flying through the air and into Joy. The whole world seemed to turn upside down. The lighting in the back of the ambulance failed and Burt lay dazed and confused in a heap on top of Joy as the ambulance slid on its side and came to a halt.

"Jesus Christ what the hell happened?!" Burt yelled through the thin wall that separated him from the driver's cab.

"Jeffrey! You okay up there? What'd you hit? Jeffrey?" There were banging noises and muffled cries coming from the cab.

"Hey Jeffrey! Damn it!"

Burt stood up and attempted to orient himself in the darkness. Unbeknownst to him he was standing on the side of the ambulance. He began feeling his way along what he believed to be the wall when he tripped over the gurney Joy had been sitting on and nearly fell forwards. Just then something in the darkness grabbed him and pulled him down. Confused, Burt pushed himself free and attempted to stand only to be felled again by unseen hands.

"Joy, stop it! Let go! I'm trying to get us out of....*AHHGGGGG*!"

Burt's sentence ended with a blood-curdling scream as Joy bit through his pants and tore out a chunk of his calf muscle. He kicked at her with his other foot and then scrambled toward the rear of the ambulance. Burt threw open the door and fell out onto the pavement. Not wanting to take his eyes off the back of the ambulance, he rolled onto his back and started dragging himself away. That was when he noticed them.

Seemingly injured people were clambering onto the wrecked ambulance. In his panic-stricken state, he mistakenly assumed that they were victims of the crash. Burt called out to them for help before he saw Jeffrey in their midst, holding his bloody throat with one hand while trying to fend them off with the other. The look on Jeffrey's face was pure terror. He was trying to scream but only gurgling sounds were coming out. Several of them stopped their attack on Jeffrey and began closing in on Burt. To his horror, he saw that the people still surrounding his friend were biting mouth-sized portions of flesh from his body.

"Oh shit! Get away from me! Help! Get away! What do you want? Help! Somebody help!"

Burt resembled a crab trying to scuttle away from a flock of seagulls on the beach as he tried to put more distance between himself and the approaching menace. Joy caught his eye as she stepped out of the ambulance. He hesitated briefly before resuming his backwards crawl. He couldn't help staring at her. She was as beautiful as she was horrible to look at. In the pale light of the setting full moon, he could see the seductive curves of her body. He could also see the dark blood that covered her ample chest and the purplish veins that traversed her neck and face as she moved closer to him.

"Stop! Get away!"

Burt flipped onto his belly and scrambled to a nearly standing position before Joy caught up with him. She grabbed his arm and spun him around. With a loud whack, she slapped him hard across the face.

"Run," she slurred in a deep, raspy voice that didn't seem to belong to a woman.

"What?"

"Run!" she screamed with her eyes pinched shut and her face contorted in a hideous snarl.

Burt was momentarily stupefied but quickly regained his senses and rapidly began hobbling away, stealing glances over his shoulder as he went. What he saw amazed him. Joy, half-naked and injured, was single-handedly taking on a mob of lunatics and she was kicking ass. Awful screams and snapping sounds echoed behind him. He'd never heard anything like it. He couldn't tell if they were from Joy but the unnatural screams made the hair on the back of his neck stand up.

Burt limped on into the early hours of the morning before he finally collapsed in the sand. He was breathing so hard that he couldn't tell if anyone had been following him and to make matters worse a thick fog was setting in.

*When the hell does it ever get foggy in a freakin' desert?* Burt lamented.

He had no idea how long it had been since the attack but he was exhausted and his leg was killing him. Burt told himself he would only rest long enough to get his strength back. Nevertheless, he desperately needed to find the Highway again. There were no landmarks in the desert for him to position himself and he had been too scared to remember that he should count his paces. The paramedic silently berated himself for not paying attention to where he was running. He had tried to cut back toward where he thought the Highway should be but it wasn't there. Now he had the nagging feeling that he had been traveling in a big circle. He thought that once or twice, he might've run across a dirt road but in the unnatural fog it was hard to tell.

Burt closed his eyes and listened, hoping to hear the noise of traffic somewhere in the distance. The dense fog muffled sounds so that all he heard was an annoying ringing in his ears and his pounding heart.

*Damn, no cars...nothing. Crap, maybe I'll wait here until it starts getting light out. I can't see where I'm going.*

Burt leaned over, touched his wounded calf and grimaced.

*I can't believe she bit me...bitch. And what the hell was wrong with those... people? Bunch of freakin' meth-heads. God...what if they had somthin'...they looked like freakin' zombies!*

"Wish I'd had a gun," he growled.

He was lost in his thoughts when he heard the distinct sound of sagebrush crunching. Burt's head shot straight up and his heart started to race. Although every fiber of his being was telling him to bolt like a frightened rabbit, he sat quietly without moving a muscle. He heard the noise again, and again. Something was definitely moving around out there. Burt thought that if he remained perfectly still whatever it was might just move on past him. The seconds dragged on for an eternity before he finally saw a figure materialize out of the fog in front of him. It was still too far away to resolve any detail but from its size, he surmised it was a man. Still it came closer and closer. Sweat poured down Burt's face even though the moist desert air was nearly freezing. He tried to swallow but couldn't. His throat was too dry. This was maddening, the fear, and the torture of not knowing who or what was out there. Burt was at his wits end. He couldn't stand it any longer.

He jumped up and screamed, "What do you want from me!"

At nearly the same time, Jeffrey Moore stumbled out of the darkness and collapsed into Burt's arms.

"Jeffrey! Oh God! I thought you were…they were all over you! I'm sorry man. I wanted to help. Jeffrey?" Burt moaned.

Jeffrey gurgled something unintelligible.

"Oh man, what'd they do to you?" Burt asked then began to sob uncontrollably.

He'd been a paramedic long enough to know that Jeffrey wasn't going to make it. He cradled his friend in his arms and rocked him back and forth on his knees while tears streamed down his face. Within a few seconds, Jeffrey went limp. There was nothing Burt could do. Jeffrey's throat had been ripped out. It was a miracle that he had made it this far. Burt refused to look down at him. Instead, he kept rocking him, telling him everything was going to be all right.

"You and me, we'll go to the Bahamas. I've got this place picked out. You remember the one we talked about? We'll sit on the beach…order drinks, check out the hot babes… kick back…. relax. You won't have to worry about a thing."

After a few minutes, Burt finally laid his friend down in the sand and stood up. The Eastern horizon was just beginning to show the dim, bluish glow that announced the coming of the dawn. Burt knew if he traveled toward that glow he would eventually hit HWY 40 or one of the other access roads heading to Flagstaff, Arizona. Judging by when their ambulance had crashed he guessed that he was a little more than halfway there. He wiped his face on the back of his hand and stared into the blackness. He didn't want to stay in this place any longer. He wanted to be anywhere other than here. Searching the horizon, his spirits lifted when he saw a dim light twinkling in the distance.

"Yes, a house!"

He turned to take one last look at his friend before he set off into the desert only to find that he had vanished. At first, Burt thought his eyes were playing tricks on him or that he just wasn't looking in the right place. But then he walked over to the spot where he was sure that he'd laid his friend and there was nothing there. He looked up and swung his head quickly from side to side, scanning the night for Jeffrey.

"Jeffrey? Hey, you out there? Jeffrey?" he called in a loud whisper.

He was suddenly overcome with a feeling of impending doom.

"Screw this. I'm out of here," Burt said under his breath.

As he turned to leave, he walked right into Jeffrey and inhaled loudly with fright.

"Jesus you scared me! I thought you were dead!"

Jeffrey lunged at Burt and sank his teeth into his throat before he could scream, ripping out soft flesh and artery alike. Wide-eyed and terrified, Burt stumbled back a few feet before falling to the ground. In a futile attempt to stop the bleeding, he grasped his torn throat with both hands as his life pumped out onto the sand.

Burt's last words bubbled out thick with blood, *"Godblllugh! Helpbllugh!"*

Jeffrey watched the pitiful scene without remorse until Burt stopped twitching. Then he turned slowly toward the tiny little light in the distance and started walking.

Joy stood beside the overturned ambulance surveying the carnage she'd wrought. Corpses and mangled pieces of them lay everywhere. Tendrils of cool, glowing mist had snaked among them and coalesced into a solid blanket covering the dead like a white sheet in a morgue. She didn't know what'd been wrong with them but felt certain it was the same disease that had taken Roy from her.

*So that's what I'm going to become ...disgusting. Some of them looked dead before I killed them...but that could not be. There are no such things as zombies,* she thought.

Even through the cobwebs in her head, she knew that she'd attacked Burt and had tried to atone for it by staying behind and slaughtering every last thing that moved while he ran away. It was only a matter of time now before she ended up like the sheriff. Even in the fading moonlight, she could see the ugly purple veins standing out against her own flesh. Joy began to realize this thing; this disease infecting people was more than just some violence-causing virus. But she was having trouble thinking. She just couldn't focus on anything and the strangest feeling was coursing through her body. It was as if tiny needles were jabbing her extremities causing all her muscles to continually twitch. But something else was bothering her. After all the fighting, Joy was startled to discover that she wasn't even breathing hard. Panic set in as she became increasingly paranoid that she might not be breathing at all. She started hyperventilating and clutched her chest only to find something even more disturbing. The familiar drumming beneath her breast wasn't there. In its place were only a few sporadic thumps from somewhere deep inside.

"What's happening to me?" Joy asked the night sky.

As if in answer to her question, all at once her body began to spasm from her eyelids down to her toes. These soon gave rise to convulsions that caused her teeth to chatter together so hard that they began breaking. Her transformation was well underway. Joy collapsed to the ground and thrashed wildly like a fish out of water. In the back of her mind she knew something awful was taking place but was powerless to stop it. Joy took center-stage as the unwilling performer in death's grand symphony, all the dreadful movements of which flowed fluidly and horribly from one into the next. She threw her head back and howled in agony as her spine arched into a perfect bow accompanied by dreadful popping sounds and the steady flopping of her legs against the ground. During this time, all the waste in her body exited uncontrollably onto the sand. Joy's arms shot straight out behind her, flipping her onto her stomach while becoming grossly hyper-extended at the elbows. Her hands bent downward sharply at the wrists and her fingers curled inward on themselves like dying maple leaves. Abruptly her jaws slammed shut, aborting a scream that was at full volume. Bloody froth bubbled out from around her broken teeth, which were now firmly embedded in her nearly severed tongue. Joy's eyes bulged out of their sockets until all the capillaries burst, staining the whites of her eyes crimson. Those bloody eyes continued staring helplessly into the fog, slowly becoming devoid of any thought or emotion. Joy was the most vulnerable a human being could be.

The deputy's body lay in that rigid position for quite some time before it finally relaxed allowing her head to slump forward. Her long brown hair spilled around her form onto the desert. She was a corpse floating face down in a sea of sand.

# NERVES

**November 29:**

Jake Northrop gathered everybody together in the outer lab to address his discoveries made during Chris' autopsy. The sun was already rising and nobody had slept. He knew he had to keep this brief or risk alienating them further.

"I've learned several things tonight. First of all, either this disease spreads much faster than anything I'm familiar with or people are getting infected by means other than direct contact with bodily fluids," Jake explained.

"Like how? Why didn't he look sick? Why didn't she look sick?" Shams asked while pointing to the room where Jennifer was resting.

"I'm getting to that. Chris said he was bitten four days ago. Jennifer was bitten maybe a day ago at the most. But judging from the extent of her disease I'd say she's had it for weeks. Maybe her boyfriend infected her. Maybe one of the animals here in the lab infected her. I don't know."

"Idiot! And you brought us back here! For what, so we could be exposed to your sick guinea pigs? I for one don't want any part of it!" Jameson snapped at Jake.

"You're free to leave. But if you want to stay, you'll do what I tell you," Jake enunciated the words clearly and carefully, first pointing to the door and then to Jameson.

Jameson glared at Jake for a few seconds and then finally looked down at the floor and snorted.

"As I was saying, I isolated some of the bacteria and noted the time it took for them to complete cell division. This is called generation time. They divide much faster than the bacteria I engineered. They've changed ... mutated somewhat, but that's not really all that uncommon for bacteria. Under normal circumstances, bacterial generation time could be as little as fifteen minutes or it could take several days, depending on the species. The generation time for the bacteria responsible for this disease is right at four and a half minutes. Now that's a lot faster than they were replicating before but still not fast enough to do what we've been seeing."

"What the hell are you talkin' bout Doc?" Bill asked.

"Let me explain. From what I've seen the bacteria quickly coat and then replace nerve and muscle cells throughout the body, starting with the brain."

"How long does this take Doc?"

"Well, all together the nerve bundles comprising our spines are on the average of eighteen inches long. Each of these bacteria infecting us is tiny, only around one micron long. But under ideal conditions even normal bacteria could cover the length of a human spinal cord in a little as fifty days. The ones causing this disease seem to be able to do it in just under four."

"I still don't see what you're getting at." Shams replied.

Jake stared into the faces of the people before him, his eyes passing quickly over each of them. He clearly saw their concern and felt a sudden wave of sympathy at their inability to understand the ramifications of his findings. He was a professor and it was his job to help people understand that which eluded them. To this end, Jake decided to honor his profession and teach.

"We have somewhere in the neighborhood of forty five miles worth of nerve cells in our bodies, that is if you string them all end to end. You see bacterial growth is exponential, one makes two, two makes four and so on. But even exponential bacterial growth can't account for what I've seen in these people. It'd take a hell of a lot longer than four days to cover that kind of real-estate."

Confused, Mary asked, "Well then what are you saying?"

"Don't you get it? I'm saying that Chris, Jennifer, Blaine, and anybody who's become one of those things have been infected for a long time," Jake said, exasperatedly.

"No, I don't get it. You're not making any sense. First, you said this stuff grows really fast. But what are you saying now, that it's not responsible for the zombies?" Mary asked.

"Do you have any idea how annoying your voice is right now, at this very minute?"

Mary was taken aback by Jake's statement and her mouth dropped open in disbelief. Clearly, she was not used to being talked to in that manner. It was the effect he was going for. Jake turned toward the others and tried to make them understand.

"No, no that's not what I'm saying. Look guys, I'm pretty sure the bacteria are causing all this but they're not doing it in four days. These people have been infected for a lot longer than that. It must lie dormant until something happens to initiate the later-stage symptoms. This stuff....these bacteria are all around us now. They're in the soil. I engineered them from garden-variety bacteria for God's sake. They can survive just about anywhere. They could be on the surface of things we touch. They could be anywhere by now. Chris, Jennifer...they might've even ingested them."

Jake slapped a mosquito on his neck and looked thoughtfully at the bloody smear on his hand before he solemnly declared, "They could've been injected with them."

At once, everyone began talking over each other, asking Jake questions.

"How do you know its everywhere? How do you know?" Shams asked.

"Wait, are you telling me that any of us could turn into one of those damned things at any time?" Bill asked.

"Why didn't you tell us this before? We could've been using hand sanitizer or..."

Jake interrupted Mary in the middle of her monologue, "Hey, listen. Give me a second to answer okay? First of all it's like I said, I made this stuff out of common soil bacteria."

"Why would you make something like that? Why?"

"I've already told you! I didn't make it so it would infect people! It wasn't supposed to do that. When I was working with the rabbits, it could only infect them so long as they were on immunosuppressant drugs! I don't know what happened. Shams I've tested surfaces here in the lab and it's all over the place. It's everywhere! It's all over us. Most of that's from fighting those things but its *e v e r y w h e r e  o k a y?*" Jake yelled the last part until he was red in the face.

Shams looked nervously at the others before replying, "Okay."

"How long do we got, Doc?"

Jake looked at Bill and then around at the rest of the frightened group and shook his head.

"I don't know. I guess it's really going to depend on how long each of us has been infected. Like with any bacterial infection each person's reaction may be different. Some of us may only be carriers. It's hard to say."

"Guess," Bill demanded.

"A few days, maybe weeks if we're lucky."

# THE KING OF EVERYTHING

**November 29**
**Market Street Tunnel, Center City:**

Ruben stood over Carl's limp body and began kicking him in the side.

"Hey you, wake up! Wake up! What's your name?" Ruben growled in a voice that was an odd mix of dry-rotted rope pulled through a hole in a dusty wooden plank and the labored, bubbling, breathing of an asthmatic with bronchitis.

Carl moaned but never opened his eyes. Ruben tilted his head slightly and squinted. He studied Carl for a moment and then knelt beside his new toy. He grabbed a handful of Carl's hair and pulled his head backward to get a better look at his face. He was having trouble seeing in the dim light and had to get right in front of his plaything to focus. With his other rotting hand he opened one of Carl's eyes and stared into it as if expecting to see something of great importance.

"I know you're in there. Come out in play-ay!" Ruben said in a sing-song cadence.

"Hey! Hey!" Ruben shouted as he slapped Carl's face repeatedly.

"Ahhhhh, useless piece of meat!" Ruben raged when Carl failed to respond.

He threw Carl's head down hard against the cold, wet concrete and kicked him over onto his side. Ruben was still a little surprised at his newfound strength and smiled knowing he could snap bone with his bare hands. As his rage subsided, Ruben's attention quickly focused on something sticking out of Carl's back pocket.

"What do we have here, a wallet? Hmmm, maybe I'll get an answer from you, useless piece of…." Ruben mumbled.

He thumbed through the wallet and found a picture of a woman that looked somewhat familiar to him. It was Heather, but he didn't know it yet. Only minutes before he'd locked a woman that looked just like her in a vault at the other end of the tunnel. Ruben had found her on the way back from University City. She was stumbling around in the tunnels. Unlike other undead things he'd run across, she seemed to retain a little bit of who she used to be. He thought they might make good companions since they were unique. But she was afraid of him when she realized he was... different. This really pissed him off so he locked her away.

He frowned at the fuzzy picture wondering if it was indeed the same woman. When he flipped back to the driver's license in the wallet understanding dawned on him.

"You! You're the doctor that treated me before all this happened! And that woman, that's... the nurse? Oh you've got to be kidding me! You and her? Ha-ha-ha-ha-HAAA! Oh this is too good! This is destiny!" he grinned malevolently and threw his head back laughing as he clapped his decaying hands together.

Ruben squinted at the driver's license, "You know Carl I think this is the start of a beautiful relationship. I have so many things to show you, wonderful things! Things you've never imagined. And we'll begin soon...very soon. But for now I have some work to do and you my friend need to stay alive a little while longer. Soon Carl, very soon."

He stood up and walked out of the room, cackling as he latched the heavy iron door to the bank vault.

Ruben walked through the condemned tunnels beneath the bank. This part of the building had been closed off for years and forgotten about. He'd accidentally found this place while he was still among the living. The old tunnels beneath the city formed a labyrinth that he'd come to know well. He could move undetected from one building in University City to another clear across town in Center City. Here he had worked in secret, growing his own variety of the professor's bacteria. He'd hoped to sell it to other bioengineering companies for a hefty profit but nothing had gone right. The only taker had been Krattatech Industries and they didn't give him half of what it was worth. And then he'd gotten sick and everything changed. The way Jennifer had looked at him for the first time after his transformation felt as if alcohol had been poured on his razor-burned soul. He tried to make her understand, tried to make her see the person underneath the rotting flesh but she rejected him, the world rejected him. He'd forced himself upon her to no avail. His old body didn't work that way anymore. It was pathetic really.

"Damn her!" Ruben shouted to himself as he walked through the dank, dark tunnel.

He had lost everything, his girlfriend, his dreams, and his life. He was angry at first, angry at the world and he just needed revenge. He wanted someone, Jake Northrop, anyone to pay for the fate that had befallen him. But the very person responsible for all his problems had been killed, taken away from him before he could exact his revenge.

"Bastards!" he yelled into the tunnel.

Ruben continued reminiscing as he trudged through the unholy passageway. It wasn't fair. Now that he had no purpose, what was he to do, rot away?

*No! That's what the world wants! Ruben Stanley is not about to give up!*

He might've lost everything that life had to offer but now he had a new outlook on things. He'd found Carl and the nurse. Once again, he had a purpose. Ruben's face twisted into a semblance of a smile as he continued his underground stroll.

"What's the one thing uniting all rulers, Kings, Presidents, and despots alike?" he asked the darkness.

"Power," he answered and laughed maniacally.

His laughter stopped abruptly when he ran directly into a wall he should've easily avoided. It didn't hurt at all. It was just the sudden shock of something immoveable in front of him that was a surprise. Ruben reached up to his eyes and realized he could barely see his hand. Only when he shined the flashlight directly on it, could he see and even then it was if he were looking through a glass of milky water. He'd begun noticing his failing vision days ago but hadn't given it too much thought before now. Ruben growled and started looking around the tunnel frantically. How could he carry out his plans with no sight? He was vulnerable and afraid.

*What a cruel joke this is, trapped inside this rotting hulk!*

In a fit of madness, Ruben began tearing away the decaying flesh of his arms only to meet rather formidable resistance well before he hit bone.

*What's this?* He asked himself while staring at the silky-black substance.

He knew the bacteria had colonized and even replaced his own nervous system but had no idea it'd replaced muscle tissue as well.

"Of course! I should've known!"

Suddenly filled with a glimmer of hope, he reached down into his pants and tore at the putrid penis in his shorts.

"No… *No! Arrrgggg!"* he screamed when the rotting flesh came off in his hands leaving behind a stringy, blackish-green mess resembling pumpkin innards.

He threw it on the ground and stepped back away from the thing as if it were going to attack him. In his hope for salvation, he'd forgotten his human anatomy lessons. There are no muscles in the male organ, only nerves, blood vessels, and spongy tissue.

There he was underground in his catacombs, dead and yet somehow alive. Ruben Stanley stared at the very thing that had made him a man, now lying in a disgusting pile on the cold ground and he was separated from it forever. He howled at the top of his lungs and clenched his fists together tightly causing the fingernails to peel off. He could take no more of this anguish. Ruben opened his hands and looked at them briefly before plunging his rotting fingers into his eyeballs. They burst easily like two overripe plums, spilling putrid slime down his face. Screaming insanely, he ran through the tunnels tripping over himself every few feet until a voice brought him back from the brink of madness.

"Hey buddy, you ok?"

Ruben jerked his head toward the sound expecting more darkness…but he could see and what he saw was astonishing. It was like looking at a black & white 35 mm film-negative, but different. Ruben pulled away the remaining slimy chunks of eyeball and stared in amazement. The man in front of him seemed to glow without any outside illumination. Ruben was seeing infrared light. He could even see the footprints the man left as he walked toward him. What's more, Ruben realized the man couldn't see him, not yet anyway. If he had, surely he would've run away in horror. Ruben reacted quickly.

"Yeah, I'm ok. Just had something in my eyes but I'm better now," Ruben said in a menacing voice that was meant to be reassuring.

"The way you were hollerin' back there…scared the crap outta me. Are you sure you're ok buddy? I can't see you in the shadows…why don't you come over here and take a drink with me huh? It gets kinda lonely down here you know," the old man said as he walked toward his little pile of burning twigs.

Ruben considered leaving the old man alone to die from his vice but thought better of it. Besides, he needed recruits for his army if he were going to be the King of Everything.

# LOVED ONES

**November 29**
**Potter Field Laboratory:**

Jake turned to address the group and held up a cloudy, reddish-looking liquid in a clear plastic vial.

"I'm sure Bill told you about the antibiotics I've prepared. I want everyone here to start taking them. Each of these tubes holds about a tablespoon. I've made a sufficient quantity for everybody to get a full course of treatment. I don't want to get your hopes up too high. This might not cure us but it'll certainly slow down the disease."

Jameson started to protest but remembered Jake's earlier warning and quickly shut his mouth. Instead, he stared bitterly at Jake and then raised his hand, all the while turning red with embarrassment.

"Yes Jameson," Jake smirked.

"I'm not taking that crap! How do we know this isn't one of your cockamamie experiments? For all I know you're trying to poison us. Why should we trust you? I'm not taking that, you hear? I'm not. None of you should either," Jameson said, pointing to everyone in the room.

"Shouldn't we wait until we talk to the CDC? Bill said you're going to tell them what happened. I mean, what if they already have something that can help us? Shouldn't we wait and see?" Mary asked.

"I wasn't going to say anything just yet but I might as well tell you now. I couldn't get through to them. All I got was a busy signal, same thing with 911. I tried calling some friends of mine at other Universities with no luck. It did get through to somebody's voice mail and I left a message but... it doesn't look good."

"Oh that's rich, that's just great. We're supposed to believe..."

Jake shot Jameson an angry look that immediately silenced him. Jameson gritted his teeth and turned redder than before. He rolled his eyes and let out a quick snort before raising his hand again.

"Yes Jameson?"

"We're supposed to believe you tried to call them? How stupid do you think we are anyway?"

"Go ahead, try your phones people. See if you have any luck. I'll wait," Jake retorted as he held out his hand pretending to examine his fingernails.

"I've been trying to call my mom in Denver but I can't get through,' said Mary.

"Nothing," Shams added.

"Now that you see I'm not making this up; we can get started with the treatments."

"What is that stuff you want us to take?" asked Shams.

"It's a combination of nanoparticle-bound, broad-spectrum antibiotics used to treat MRSA, mainly vancomycin and linezolid. The bacteria will attempt to metabolize the iron-oxide nanoparticles and in doing so, they will encounter the antibiotics. It should be a perfect delivery system to slow them down."

"Wait, aren't those the antibiotics they *used* to treat superbugs with? Didn't they quit working though? Isn't that why they don't use them anymore?" Mary asked.

"No they're just not as effective against antibiotic-resistant infections as they used to be," explained Jake.

"Let me get this straight, Doc. You want us to drink some rusty ole tap water with outdated meds in it?" asked Bill.

"If you have a better idea I'd love to hear it."

Bill peered at Jake with a mixture of hatred and respect before he spat his reply, "Well I do. I'm goin' down the street and find me a liquor store. You can shove your rust water where the sun don't shine."

"Wait up I'm going with you!" Jameson shouted as he darted out of the lab after Bill.

Mary kept looking nervously back and forth between Jake and the rapidly departing pair.

"Are you going to just let them leave?" Shams asked.

"They're grown men. They can make their own decisions."

"What if more of those things come back? We will need them! You should stop them," Shams implored.

"I should stop them?" Jake asked incredulously.

He walked over to Shams and stood inches from his face.

"Give me one good reason!" Jake yelled.

"You said you would help us."

"I tried to help you! I tried to help all of you but no one listens! Why don't you stop them? Better yet, why don't you leave too! Both of you! Get out of here!" Jake ranted as he pointed toward the door.

"Come on Shams. Let's go," Mary said as she locked arms with Shams and led him out of the lab. Shams kept looking back over his shoulder at the professor with a look of disappointment as he walked.

Jake stood in the doorway to the lab and watched as the two of them rounded the corner.

"Don't come back either! Bunch of parasites!" fumed Jake.

Jake re-entered the lab and began gathering together equipment he thought he might need. Furiously he began throwing mixing cups, syringes, and jars of powder into a heap. He grabbed a box containing a tranquilizer dart and was about to toss it over his shoulder and onto the pile of supplies when a sudden noise behind him made him stop moving. Without turning around, he began speaking.

"I thought I told you not to come back."

A familiar voice replied, "Where the hell's my daughter!"

Jake spun around, "Ron? Man am I glad to see you!"

"Shut up! She told me she'd be here now - where is she?" Ron shouted, on the verge of madness.

The sweat that ran down the sides of his face left flesh-colored tracks through the grime. His white dress shirt was untucked and there were filthy handprints on both sides it. In his shaking hand was a chrome-plated revolver, pointed at Jake.

"Ron, just calm down and let me explain."

"No! No! I've had enough of your explanations! This, all of this is your fault isn't it? Oh yeah, this reeks of you Northrop! Everything that's happened is because of you!" Ron screamed and gesticulated wildly, inscribing first a large arc with his free hand and then jabbing his gun at Jake.

"Just wait a minute! I'm trying to tell you…"

*Bang!* A gunshot cut Jake's explanation short as a fluid-filled flask beside him exploded, covering everything with glass and chemicals.

"One more word out of you and I'll pop a cap in your…"

"Daddy?" Jennifer asked as she stumbled into the outer lab.

Ron immediately lowered his weapon and ran over to his daughter. He grabbed her up in his arms and kissed her cheek.

"Oh baby, are you alright? You don't look so good. Daddy's got you. It's all right. Come on now, I'll take you home."

"Ron, I wouldn't do that if I were you. She…"

"You! I'm not finished with you Jake! When this is over I'll see to it that you never work anywhere near a University again!"

Jennifer's legs buckled and Dr. Langley had to support all her weight.

"You don't understand. She needs…"

"Enough! Just leave us alone!" Dr. Langley screamed.

Powerless to stop them, Jake stood trembling with frustration as he watched Ron drag Jennifer out of his lab. When they were out of sight, he walked over to the pile of medical equipment that he'd hastily assembled and began kicking it across the room. He flopped down in the middle of it and put his face in his hands. Ice water filled his heart when suddenly he heard the telltale hiss of the re-animated reverberating down the hall. He could hear Ron pleading as well. Jake jumped to his feet, grabbed a shovel, and burst out of the lab, running toward Ron's voice.

"No baby not you. *Not you….* Please don't do this to me God, not my baby please," Dr. Langley begged as tears and sweat rolled down his face.

Jennifer was on her feet staggering toward her father. Ron was slowly backing up, pistol in his shaking hand.

"Don't come any closer baby… please. I can get you help," sobbed Ron.

"Don't come any…"

*Bang!* Ronald Langley accidentally pulled the trigger. A single bullet ripped through Jennifer's abdomen and spattered gore onto the wall behind her. Dr. Langley gasped and put his hand over his mouth in shock as his daughter fell to the floor.

Almost immediately, he tore his hand away and yelled her name, "Jennifer! No!"

He took a few steps toward his daughter lying on the floor and then stopped. Trembling all over, Ron stared at the large bloody hole in her back. He turned robotically toward Jake with a blank expression on his face and put the gun to his temple.

For Jake Northrop, everything appeared to happen in slow motion.

"Ron don't!" he screamed an instant before brains and tufts of hair splattered all over the wall on the other side of Dr. Langley.

Jake didn't even hear the gun go off. He was still screaming Ron's name when his boss' lifeless body crumpled to the floor. With a throat too dry to scream any more, Jake ran his hands through his hair and down the front of his face, stretching the flesh away from his eyes and distorting his appearance. None of this was supposed to happen. Jake's whole world was a maddening hell.

Movement on the floor caused him to quickly step back against the wall. Jennifer was pulling herself up on her hands and knees. She raised her head and looked at Dr. Langley' corpse. She crawled over to him and put her hand on his cheek. After a moment, she laid her head on his chest and hugged him as any child would hug their father.

Jake was puzzled by Jennifer's behavior and felt compelled to attempt communication with her. Unsure of the outcome, he kept his distance and made sure there was a clear getaway in case things went badly. As delicately as possible, Jake said her name and then braced for her reaction. A few seconds went by and still she'd not reacted. Jake inhaled deeply and said her name again, this time a little louder and with more authority. There was still no reaction from her. Jake began to consider the possibility that she might've been human when Ron shot her and that she might've, in fact, just died. It was a horrible scenario that he judged unlikely given the progression of her illness. He recalled the throaty sounding hiss he'd heard earlier and knew it could mean only one thing. Jake took a few short steps toward Jennifer and, blinking his eyes rapidly, steadied himself for what may come. Right on cue, the lights began to flicker as if some supernatural force had entered the hallway. Jake gripped the shovel like a baseball bat and nervously twisted his hands back and forth in opposite directions around the thick wooden handle.

"Jennifer! Can you..."

Seeming possessed, Jennifer's prostrate form leapt into the air and spun around to face Jake. Landing in a three-point-stance and growling like a rabid dog, the creature was a gross caricature of an offensive lineman. Its purplish-green face twisted into a sardonic snarl while long strings of bloody slobber spilled from its mouth and chin. Jake instinctively backed up and prepared to swing his shovel.

"Wait Jennifer, don't you know who I am?" Jake implored.

*"Yoouuu did thisss!"* hissed the creature in a gravelly, mucous-laden voice.

The thing threw its head back, roared something unintelligible, and charged Jake. He had no choice. Jake swung the straight-bladed shovel directly into Jennifer's face.

*Thwang!* With a loud ringing crack, steel met flesh and bone.

As the thing fell, Jake saw the distorted features of a face he'd once known and cared about. Breathing heavily, he stood over Jennifer's broken figure holding his blood-soaked shovel. The thing began to move feebly and this enraged him.

"You are not my student! You are not...my...student!"

He raised his shovel and brought it down upon the creature again and again, squashing its head like an overripe watermelon. Blood and brains covered him from head to toe. Still he attempted to raise the shovel for another blow but his muscles had forsaken him and he toppled over onto the pile of goo he was intent on destroying. He had begun weakly punching at it with his fists when he heard a rather unrefined voice interrupt his self-indulgence.

"You 'bout done with that Doc? Looks like she ain't gettin' back up."

Totally spent, Jake rolled off the creature and onto his back, letting his arms flop out by his sides. He turned his head toward Bill and raised his middle finger in a vulgar gesture. Bill chuckled and offered him his hand. Scowling, Jake lay still for a moment before grabbing Bill's arm who then quickly hauled him to his feet.

"Looks like you could use somthin' to take the edge off," Bill said as his hand disappeared into his Jacket pocket and re-emerged with a bottle of rum.

Without saying anything, Jake accepted it from Bill and took a long pull from the bottle.

Bill nodded his head down the hall and said, "The others are waitin' outside. It's a nice day, sun's out and everything. Of course, Jameson has been complainin' about feelin' feverish. He's always complainin' about somthin' though."

"I thought you left for good."

Bill grinned at Jake and said, "Maybe I should've. I told you I was goin' to the store. I never said I what'n comin' back. Besides, I kinda want to see how this whole mess turns out. And you… you need someone watchin' your back. You keep gettin' yourself into trouble when I'm not around."

Jake handed the half-empty bottle of rum to Bill and began walking down the hall.

"You shouldn't have come back," Jake said without turning around.

"Now you hold on a minute Doc! Things got outta hand earlier that's all. We're in this together. We need each other!"

Jake stopped and turned around to face Bill before saying, "Looks like you have what you need," and then continued on down the hall.

Bill looked at the liquor bottle in his grimy hand and then at Jake's back. Anger that boiled within him quickly spilled over like milk from a saucepan on high heat. He threw the bottle as hard as he could at Jake's disappearing figure. It crashed against the wall beside the professor and showered him with glass and rum.

"Walk away you coward!"

"What'd you say to me you son of a…?" Jake asked ominously as Bill started talking over him.

"Where do you think you're goin'? You got people right here that need your help and you can't even bring yourself to do that! But you're gonna save the world! Save faceless people that can't look you in the eye and tell you when you're wrong or being an ass! Coward!"

Jake was walking briskly toward Bill who was walking just as fast to meet him.

"We're about to have one helluva good fight," he spat.

"I doubt it," Bill quipped acidly.

Just then, gunshots erupted from outside followed by a loud explosion that rocked the entire building.

"What the hell was that?" asked Jake.

"Sounds like the Calvary's here."

"I guess we'll have to finish this later," Jake said disappointed.

Bill quickly jabbed Jake in the face and knocked him on his butt.

"Don't be disappointed Doc. Now you got somethin' to look forward to."

Jake lay there in disbelief with his eyes rolling around as Bill once again reached out his arm to Northrop. When Jake came to his senses, he slapped Bill's hand away and stood on his own, blood pouring out of both nostrils.

"That's the spirit!" Bill said, grinning.

"This isn't obber," Jake spluttered his muffled response through bloody hands covering his nose.

"Oh I hope not," Bill replied as he jogged toward the exit.

The two men burst out of the building just in time to see zombies being cut down by Shams and the others.

"Where'd they come from?" Bill barked as he aimed his own rifle at the slowly approaching crowd of undead.

"I don't know they just started showing up!" Mary yelled back.

"That sounded like an R.P.G. a minute ago!" Bill shouted.

"A what?" Shams asked while leaning toward Bill.

"Rocket propelled grenade!" Bill yelled over the clack-clack-clack of the assault rifles.

"Someone else is shooting a few blocks over! Look over there! See!" Mary yelled.

"I see!" Bill answered.

"Get back inside! Everybody, now!" Jake commanded.

"Maybe they can help us!" Mary said.

"We don't know who they are! If we saw them, then they've seen us too! Get inside! Jameson let's go! Move it!

As usual, Jameson took his time and was the last to make inside the building. "Grab the door and hold it!"

Jameson and Mary slammed the door shut and held onto the handle, bracing themselves against the recessed door jamb.

"Crap I can't find the key!" Jake yelled as he fumbled through his pant pocket.

"Doc you gotta hurry they're right outside the door!"

Moaning sounds and banging were coming from the other side along with the awful stench of rancid meat.

"I got it! Arrrghhh! Hold the door shut damn it I can't turn the lock!"

"We can't they're pulling on it! Oh God!" screamed Mary.

The door yanked away from her hand and the dead poured in.

# BETWEEN A ROCK AND A HARD PLACE

**December 7**
**Arizona Badlands:**

Terrell walked through the Arizona badlands with his well-trained eyes glued to the ground. His white shirtsleeves were rolled up revealing colorful tattoos on deeply bronzed skin. Folk music rang from the ear buds of his iPod and drowned out the wind whistling through the sagebrush. As he stepped around a large cactus, he tugged at the gun holster that kept digging into his shoulder. Weapons weren't usually considered tools of the trade for a paleontologist but over the years Terrell had learned to always pack heat when he went out alone. After all the craziness that had been going on lately, it was only prudent.

He paused to pull off his well-worn cowboy hat and then glanced up at the burning mid-day sun. The thermometer on his watch read well over 90° F. Before putting his hat back on, he squirted a generous amount of water from the Camelback into a blue bandana and then placed it on his head, letting the back of it hang down over his sunburned neck. Terrell tucked his walking stick under his right arm and leaned on it as he picked up the GPS that hung from his pack. He scrolled through a few screens and then punched in his coordinates. Field season had long since been over with for the University but Terrell knew what he was looking for and was determined to be the first to find it.

The paleontologist's quarry was a small Mesozoic-age dinosaur called *Coelophysis.* To be more precise, he was searching for the final resting place of these animals. But this wasn't just any bone-yard he was hunting for. This was something special, a once in a lifetime discovery if he could find it. The graveyard he sought was one of only a handful around the world where soft tissues and feathers were preserved. Years of experience and careful study of the area's geology had revealed clues to its whereabouts, just not its exact location. But he was close now and he knew it. If he could find this treasure trove it might prove once and for all that birds had descended from dinosaurs. People had argued whether such a link truly existed. Some reputable scientists had gone so far to say that birds were in fact, dinosaurs. The debate had been around for years, fueled by the famous, feathered dinosaurs of China. If he found one of the earliest known dinosaurs preserved with feathers it would seal the deal, not to mention the fact that he would become famous; at least among paleontologists.

Terrell continued his search for the precious fossils, moving along at a slow but steady pace when suddenly his eyes locked onto something that shouldn't have been there in the desert, footprints and lots of them. He immediately pulled his ear buds out of his ears and began looking around for the person that had made them. Paranoid thoughts swirled through his mind. Was this person looking for fossils too or had he himself wandered onto someone else's property and was now in danger of being shot? He grabbed his GPS, stared intently at the map, and traced his trail back through the desert. He hadn't wandered off the property after all and he had permission to be out here. That could mean only one thing. Someone else was out here illegally and that fact alone made whoever it was extremely dangerous. He had heard that this was a rumored corridor for the Mexican drug cartels.

Terrell strained his ears to try and pick up any sounds that might give him a clue to where this other person may be but all he heard was the wind. He looked down again at the footprints hoping that they were at least a few days old. Terrell knelt down, touched one of the tracks, and saw how easily his finger destroyed the hard outline of a shoe. Brushing away a biting fly from his face, he looked up ahead at the meandering footprints and saw that they crosscut tracks recently left by a small animal. Still kneeling beside the footprints, Terrell continued following the animal tracks with his eyes into the nearby sagebrush. His heart nearly leapt out of his chest when he saw a brown rabbit sitting quietly underneath the desert plant. Whoever made the tracks had passed here only a few moments ago. Terrell looked back over his shoulder and considered the long hike back to the safety of his truck. He looked again at the footprints and then up ahead toward the mesas.

"Man screw that. I ain't goin' back now," he said aloud as he stood up and unholstered his gun.

With a rustling noise, the rabbit that had been sitting quietly underneath the sagebrush darted away and startled him. In his apprehension over the stranger, he'd forgotten it was there. He breathed out slowly and lowered his weapon. Terrell took one last look behind him and then reaffirmed his decision to keep going forward. Walking as quietly as possible along the only path leading between the mesas, he was filled with an escalating sense of foreboding.

The magnificent mesas rose up into the sky on either side of the paleontologist providing a little relief from the heat of the sun. For this, he was very grateful. But soon the passage between the mesas narrowed until Terrell found himself negotiating through a slot-canyon. The lower portion of the passage was almost as wide as he was tall, but from his waist up the canyon was only slightly wider than his own body. His backpack and gun were hindrances now as they kept becoming wedged between his body and the rock. His only choice was to try and lift the heavy pack off his back and stuff the shoulder holster and gun inside of it. Then he could pull it along behind him through the passage. After several minutes of swearing and grunting, the overstuffed backpack finally fell to the canyon floor. Now he could concentrate on maneuvering between the two sandstone walls closing in on either side.

Terrell moved as carefully as possible to prevent the sharp sand grains from inflicting any more cuts to his body while holding the straps to his pack in one hand. Just when he was beginning to think that he might become stuck in this tight corridor, it opened up into a cavernous room at least fifty yards long and twenty yards wide. And unlike the slot canyon he'd just escaped from, it was illuminated by the golden sunlight pouring down from overhead. For a moment, the paleontologist stood motionless, taking in the splendid view. He marveled at the various shades of purple, red, orange, and yellow that seemed to have been infused into the rock by some mysterious and powerful magic for the very purpose of amazing him.

"Oh my God I gotta get a picture of this! This is freakin' awesome!" Terrell exclaimed with wonder.

He began foraging through the crowded backpack for his camera. Reluctantly, he tossed aside his rock hammer and then his gun before his hands finally found their prize. Terrell was only a few seconds into taking pictures when his nose caught the faintest whiff of decomposition. At first, he thought he had imagined it until the smell appeared again. He lowered his camera while his eyes searched the ground. Terrell was certain that he would see something dead lying close by. But there were only pockets of loose gravel and sand lying on the water-scoured floor of the gorge. Standing in the sunlight the paleontologist narrowed his eyes into thin slits and focused on the far end of the hollow toward one of several dark, narrow passages leading out of the room. He wondered if there was an animal in there that had fallen from the rim of the canyon and died. Terrell didn't relish the thought of having to maneuver around a bloated carcass. He stared nervously out into the great room and began to hear the wind. Terrell thought it was odd that he just now noticed it moaning through the canyon. He hadn't felt the slightest hint of a breeze since he'd started traveling between the mesas.

The paleontologist placed his camera around his neck and walked toward the far side of the hollow. He ceased thinking about dead animals and the moaning wind when he noticed the mysterious footprints again in a pocket of sand that was just large enough to record a person passing. With his heart pounding, Terrell reached for his gun and found nothing but his shirt. He turned and looked to where his backpack lay at the far end of the hollow and cursed himself for carelessly abandoning it in his rapture over the beauty of the gorge. He had started walking back to retrieve it when a ghastly sounding groan echoed from one of the passages directly behind him. He spun around like a top to face whatever was coming out of the darkness. And this time Terrell knew it wasn't the wind.

Fear bubbled up from the pit of his stomach like saltwater through the rusted deck of a sinking cargo ship. There was a buzzing sound coming out the darkened passage and it was growing louder and louder. The paleontologist's jaw dropped when he saw the figure shamble out into daylight. It was dressed in a ragged sheriff's uniform that was covered with greasy, dark stains. Flies that boiled out of the passage were concentrated around its eye-sockets and nostrils. The horrible stench of week-old road kill assaulted Terrell's senses. The thing's blotchy, greenish-gray skin was overlain with hardened rivulets of crusty, black goop reminiscent of the funk that drips from the bottom of a filthy barbeque grill. Its abdomen was horribly distended and had burst out of its shirt. It seemed that any second it would split open. As it took a step toward Terrell, the inevitable happened; the thing's stomach abruptly deflated with an explosive, ripping noise. It was accompanied by wet, splattering sounds as if chili were being poured from a large pot onto the desert floor. But the creature's stomach hadn't burst. Instead, rotting filth and piles of putrid, green intestine had forcefully exited its anus and poured out of its pant legs, some of which remained attached and trailed behind the pathetic wretch. Seemingly oblivious to this, it continued homing in on the paleontologist.

Terrell didn't understand what he was witnessing. He took a quick step backward without taking his eyes off the thing and in a bizarre twist of fate, tripped over a boulder. Terrell thrust his arm out to break his fall and unfortunately wedged it between some rocks. At the same time, all of his weight continued moving downward at a tangent to the boulders causing his forearm to snap, sending bone through flesh. Howling with pain and momentarily forgetting about the creature, he gripped his ruined arm and stared at the blood spilling out around the jagged, white bone protruding from the rubbery-looking flesh of his shattered forearm. The thing coming after him bellowed awfully and snapped at the air as it searched around for Terrell. He scrambled to his feet in shock. He ran toward his gun and tripped on top of his book bag sending waves of agonizing pain through his arm.

The creature shambled toward him much faster than a thing of decay should have.

Terrell fumbled around but couldn't grasp the gun. The creature stopped short of Terrell and snarled while shaking its head left and right.

Why it occurred is a mystery. Maybe the thing recalled memories of its former self, its last moments of tortuous clarity where it'd tried to end the pain and suffering but couldn't. Something wouldn't allow it. As the sheriff Roy Clay, he'd put the gun up to his temple, said his goodbyes and began to pull the trigger. But at the last instant his hand jerked skyward allowing the bullet to only graze his head. And now pain, only pain could the thing feel.

The creature hesitated and that was all the time Terrell needed. He found the pistol and pulled the trigger as the barrel plunged into the thing's eye socket. Rancid green gore sprayed onto the sand and the thing slumped soundlessly to the ground.

# A WORLD OF MICROORGANISMS

The world of microorganisms is not all gloom and doom. On the contrary, many microbes are quite useful to humans in a variety of different areas including: medicine, bioremediation (Lovely, 2002-03; Methé et al., 2003) and yes, nanotechnology (Sorkin et al., 2006). I have included references for you eager beavers wishing to learn more about microbes. *This list is biased toward those articles that had a direct influence on me during the writing of this book series.*

Microbes in nature are important decomposers and to some extent live in symbiosis with nearly all the known species of animals and plants. If it were not for bacteria, we could not survive. They help us to digest our food and make vitamins within our bodies. In fact, there are more bacterial cells on and within your body than there are human cells! There is even a theory that maintains that we are a product of a process called endosymbiosis. According to this theory, an anaerobic prokaryotic cell phagocytized an aerobic bacterium but couldn't digest it. The aerobic bacteria remained alive within the cell. The bacterium generated ATP that allowed the anaerobic cell to digest food aerobically. In time, the two cells couldn't live independently of one another and the aerobic bacterium eventually became a mitochondrion within the anaerobic cell (see Glossary for definitions).

**Parasite host interactions**

Some microbe-host interactions are not so benign. The most obvious effects of these bad interactions are the illness and death of infected organisms. Notwithstanding the many microorganisms that are known pathogens, there are many others that affect their hosts in subtle and yet much more frightening ways. One such parasite is the Protist *Toxoplasma gondii.* This little nasty is known to alter the behavior of rodents; causing them to lose their fear of cats and to actually become attracted to felines! In this way, the parasite can continue its life cycle when the cat eats the infected rodent.

If you want to know more about microbes and host interactions, check out the list of references at the back of this book. The following are but a few of the journal articles and books dedicated to parasitism and host behavior (Stamp, 1981; Moore, 1990; Carmichael and Moore, 1991; Berdoy, 2000; Zimmer, 2001; Flegr et al., 2003-03; Novotná, et al., 2005). ***Warning:*** *Some of this information is very technical and some of it is just downright creepy. Enjoy!*

**Fossil microbes**

The earliest evidence for life on earth is in the form of fossilized cyanobacterial colonies (blue-green algae) called stromatolites. These Archaean (> 3.5 billion yr.) organisms were photosynthetic eukaryotes. Although they are not very exciting to look at, they pumped massive quantities of oxygen into the atmosphere, which enabled continuing evolution of life on our planet. Microorganisms have since constituted the vast majority of life on earth.

**Strange bacterial mimicry**

In the early 1900's, a unique fossil site was found near the village of Messel, Germany. These 50 million year old fossils were remarkable in that even soft tissue such as skin, hair, and feathers were preserved in great detail. More incredible is that the soft tissues are reported to have been replaced by bacteria (Wuttke, 1983). However, a more recent study has demonstrated that the remains are more than likely pigment bodies called melanosomes (Vinther et. al., 2009).

At any rate, fossil locations such as the one mentioned above are uncommon but have been found all over the world. A few of these treasure troves contain soft-tissue fossils from geologic eras much farther back in time than those from Messel Germany. One such site dating back to the Mesozoic era (i.e., dinosaur-age) was discovered in the United States (Bingham et al., 2008). At this site, scientists discovered a large collection of feathers that may've belonged to dinosaurs or birds or possibly both. These feathers were found to be preserved in the same way as those mysterious fossils from Germany!

Unlike the fictional scenario presented in this book, the animals preserved in these fossil localities were quite dead before possibly being replaced by bacteria…at least so we believe.

**Aerobic:** Cellular metabolism requiring oxygen

**Anaerobic:** Cellular metabolism without oxygen

**Artificial Intelligence (A.I.):** Intelligence or iterative learning exhibited by a man-made device

**Artificial Neural Network:** A group of artificial neurons that communicate with one another to process information

**Adenosine Triphosphate (ATP):** Transports chemical energy within cells and is used as an energy source

**Bacteria:** Single-celled microorganisms "decomposers" which can exist independently or with the aid of a host

***Geobacter*:** Photosynthetic bacteria useful in the bioremediation of sites contaminated with heavy metals

**Eukaryote:** Organisms with complex cells and a membrane-bound nucleus. Most are multicellular

**Fungi:** Eukaryote "decomposers" with cell walls. They do not photosynthesize; they rely on carbon fixed by other organisms for metabolism and often form symbiotic relationships with their host

**Iteration:** Repetition

**Minsky, Marvin Lee:** Developer of the first randomly wired neural network learning machine, co-developer of the Society of Mind Theory, and co-founder of MIT's AI laboratory

**Mitochondrion:** Provide eukaryotic cells with energy (cellular power-house)

**Neural Network:** A group of interconnected neurons that define a recognizable circuit.

**Phagocytosis:** Form of feeding whereby large particles of food (cells) are enveloped by the cell membrane and internalized to form a phagosome, or food vacuole.

**Prokaryote:** Organisms without a cell nucleus, or indeed any other membrane-bound organelles, in most cases uni-cellular

**Protists:** Eukaryotes that are not animals, plants or fungi. They have no highly specialized tissues, are mostly single-celled, are motile, and feed by phagocytosis.

***Toxoplasma gondii*:** Protist (eukaryote) that suppresses the immune system and induces behavior alterations; common in felines, domestic or wild

# REFERENCES

Berdoy, M., Webster, J.P., & Macdonald, D.W., 2000, Fatal attraction in Toxoplasma-infected rats: a case of parasite manipulation of its mammalian host, Proceedings of the Royal Society (London), Series B. 267, 1591-1594

Bingham, P.S., Savrda, C.E. , Knight, T.K., Lewis, R.D., 2008, Character and Genesis of the Ingersoll Shale, A Compact Fossil-Lagerstätte, Upper Cretaceous, Eutaw Formation, eastern Alabama, Palaios, v. 23, p. 391-401.

Carmichael, L.M., and Moore, J., 1991., A Comparison of Behavioral Alterations in the Brown Cockroach, Periplaneta brunnea, and the American Cockroach, Periplaneta americana, Infected With the Acanthocephalan, Moniliformis moniliformis. Journal of Parasitology, v. 77, no. 6, p. 931-936.

Flegr, J., Preiss M., Klose, J., Havlíček, J., Vitáková, M, Kodym, P., 2003, Decreased level of psychobiological factor novelty seeking and lower intelligence in men latently infected with the protozoan parasite Toxoplasma gondii, Dopamine, a missing link between schizophrenia and toxoplasmosis, Biological Psychology, v. 63, p. 253-268.

Flegr J., Havlíček, J., Kodym, P., Malý, M., Šmahel, Z., 2002, Increased risk of traffic accidents in subjects with latent toxoplasmosis: a retrospective case-control study, BMC Infectious Diseases, v. 2, no.11, p.1-13.

Lovley, D.R., 2003, Cleaning Up With Genomics: Applying Molecular Biology to Bioremediation, Nature Reviews Microbiology v.1, p.36-44.

Lovley, D.R., 2002, Analysis of the Genetic Potential and Gene Expression of Microbial Communities Involved in the In Situ Bioremediation of Uranium and Harvesting Electrical Energy from Organic Matter, OMICS, v.6, no.4, p.331-339.

Methé, B.A. et al, 2003, Genome of Geobacter sulfurreducens: Metal Reduction in Subsurface Environments, Science v. 302, no.5652, 1967.

Moore, J. and Gotelli, N.J., 1990, A Phylogenetic Perspective on the Evolution of Altered Behaviors: a Critical Look at the Manipulation Hypothesis, In: Parasitism and Host Behavior (Ed. by C.J. Barnes and J.M. Behnke), p. 193-233. London: Taylor & Francis.

Novotná, M., Hanusova, J., Klose, J., Preiss, M., Havlicek, J., Roubalová, K., Flegr, J., 2005, Probable neuroimmunological link between Toxoplasma and cytomegalovirus infections and personality changes in the human host, BMC Infectious Diseases, v. 5, p. 54.

Sorkin, R., Gabay, T., Blinder, P., Baranes, D., Ben-Jacob, E., Hanein, Y., 2006, Compact self-wiring in cultured neural networks, Journal of Neural Engineering, v.3, p.95-101.

Stamp, N.E., 1981, Behavior of Parasitized Aposematic Caterpillars: Advantageous to the Parasitoid or the Host? The American Naturalist, v. 118, no.5, p. 715-725.

Vinther, J., Briggs, D.E., Clarke, J.C., Mayr, G., Prum, R.O., 2009, Structural Coloration in a Fossil Feather, Biology Letters, doi:10.1098/rsbl.2009.0524.

Webster, J.P., (in press), The impact of Toxoplasma infection on host behaviour, Invited review for Microbes and Infection.

Wuttke, M., 1983, 'Weichteil-Erhaltung' durch lithifizierte Mikroorganismen bei mittel-eozinen Vetebraten aus den Olschiefern der 'Grube Messel' bei Darmstadt. Senckenbergiana lethaea, v. 64, 509-527.

Zimmer, C., 2001, Parasite Rex, Simon and Schuster, p.320.

# Necrophobia

**Jack Hamlyn**

An ordinary summer's day.
The grass is green, the flowers are blooming. All is right with the world. Then the dead start rising. From cemetery and mortuary, funeral home and morgue, they flood into the streets until every town and city is infested with walking corpses, blank-eyed eating machines that exist to take down the living.

The world is a graveyard.

And when you have a family to protect, it's more than survival.

It's war.

More than 63% of people now believe that there will be a global zombie apocalypse before 2050...

So, you've got your survival guide, you've lived through the first chaotic months of the crisis, what next?
Employing real science and pioneering field work, War against the Walking Dead provides a complete blueprint for taking back your country from the rotting clutches of the dead after a zombie apocalypse.

* A glimpse inside the mind of the zombie using a team of top psychics - what do the walking dead think about? What lessons can we learn to help us defeat this pervading menace?
* Detailed guidelines on how to galvanise a band of scared survivors into a fighting force capable of defeating the zombies and dealing with emerging groups such as end of the world cults, raiders and even cannibals!
* Features insights from real zombie fighting organisations across the world, from America to the Philippines, Australia to China - the experts offer advice in every aspect of fighting the walking dead.
Packed with crucial zombie war information and advice, from how to build a city of the living in a land of the dead to tactics on how to use a survivor army to liberate your country from the zombies - War against the Walking Dead may be humanity's last chance.

Remember, dying is not an option !

***Available at www.severedpress.com, Amazon and most online bookstores***

# THE DEVIL NEXT DOOR

Cannibalism. Murder. Rape. Absolute brutality. When civilizations ends...when the human race begins to revert to ancient, predatory savagery...when the world descends into a bloodthirsty hell...there is only survival. But for one man and one woman, survival means becoming something less than human. Something from the primeval dawn of the race.

**"Shocking and brutal, The Devil Next Door will hit you like a baseball bat to the face. Curran seems to have it in for the world ... and he's ending it as horrifyingly as he can." *- Tim Lebbon, author of Bar None***

**"The Devil Next Door is dynamite! Visceral, violent, and disturbing!." *Brian Keene, author of Castaways and Dark Hollow***

**"The Devil Next Door is a horror fans delight...who love extreme horror fiction, and to those that just enjoy watching the world go to hell in a hand basket" – *HORROR WORLD***

**Available at www.severedpress.com, Amazon and most online bookstores**

grey dogs
Ian DG Sandusky

# THE GHOST TOUCHER

## Gerald Rice

"Haven't you ever picked up your keys for no reason and realized you had nowhere to go?" Israel asked. "Or picked up a pen and didn't have anything to write?"
"No," Kelly said.
"Sure you have. Everybody has. It's like having déjà vu about déjà vu."
"What?"
"You know-you remember remembering you've done a thing before, but you only remember remembering it when you're remembering it?"
"So when I'm not remembering it, I forget it?"
"You got it."
"No. No, I don't."

In a world where ghosts are an accepted reality, Stout Roost, reality star and host of the Network's The Ghost Toucher reality series has vanished. But Israel, the spiritual detective they hire, doesn't exactly have a plan to find him. Kelly Greene, a customer service rep, is tapped to assist the detective, but he quickly realizes that as far as unconventional methods go, Israel's are insane. He informs Kelly there is an afterworld and it was already populated by pesty ghosts. They also hate humans because they eventually become ghosts and are seeking a 'clean' way to exterminate us all. The two learn finding Stout is the least of their worries as they are pursued through metro-Detroit by obsessive compulsive wannabe warriors, mutants who worship an insane deity, weapons from the other side and a mysterious, perpetually pregnant, augmentative woman with a gender complex.

**Available at www.severedpress.com, Amazon and most online bookstores**

Lightning Source UK Ltd.
Milton Keynes UK
UKOW022009130212

187236UK00002B/15/P